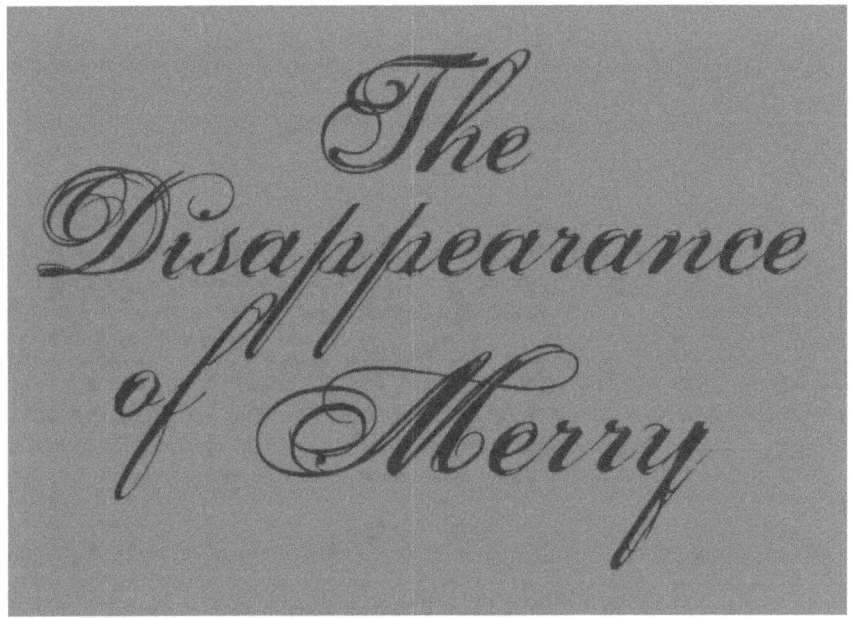

The Disappearance of Merry

VALVERDE MACLEAN

DEDICATION

To M

For being with me on the journey.

A journey far greater than we expected.

Thank you for your help, support and patience.

CONTENTS

ACKNOWLEDGMENTS

Special thanks to Sandra Fitzgerald for her kind and tactful comments on the first draft of the book. Her encouragement provided the incentive to continue the project.

My thanks to Henry and Jeanette Hauf for their comments on early drafts.

Thanks also to Lee Ord, Colleen Brady and Don Boyd. The resulting changes are of benefit to readers.

Thank you to Donna Spethman for her technical assistance, Glenda O'Sullivan for her comments on publishing, and to Annie Boyd for her encouragement and enthusiasm with writing.

Special thanks to Taylor Hyslop for his comments on cover design.

Thanks also to Natalie Harman for her suggestions on the final draft. It was greatly appreciated.

My thanks also to the staff at both the State Library of Victoria and the Central Highlands Library's Ballarat Library. Their patience and assistance during my research was much appreciated.

I would like to acknowledge the contribution of Nahum Szumer for the cover design of the book.

Lastly, thanks to Stacey Pettersson for her diligence in editing and proof-reading the penultimate draft. Her comments, wise advice and tolerance of my lapses in language and typing were greatly appreciated.. Any errors remaining are due to my subsequent alterations.

1 A CUP OF COFFEE

Suzie

There are great cups of coffee, and there are some bad cups of coffee.

Little did I know where this particular cup of coffee would take me.

I was sitting in The Tea Room at the National Gallery of Victoria cursing the fact I had worn my new heels. Style should always come second to comfort when it comes to shopping, and finding the present for my grandson's birthday had required much more walking than I had expected. Even worse I was in the wrong Gallery.

The NGV had a new exhibition on fashion, and I had decided that I would come into the city, buy Charles a present for his third birthday, and then visit the exhibition. However, on entering the Gallery on St Kilda Road, I had remembered that all the exhibitions of Australian work were now held in the new branch of the Gallery in Federation Square. I had walked close by that building on my walk from the city shops. Before I started my return to the correct Gallery I needed a coffee and to rest my feet. I wasn't sure which of these needs was most important, but the aroma of the freshly ground and brewed coffee was certainly appealing.

I wanted to see the Linda Jackson Bush Couture Exhibition. I had read a review in The Age and it looked interesting. The colours and techniques were so different to the run-of-the-mill clothing designs that filled stores and magazines. Fashion had been—well, still is—an interest of mine although I certainly don't make myself a slave to the latest look.

Then I noticed the man sitting at a table across the room from me. Nothing special, around sixty maybe, a touch of grey in the hair and a bit thin on top. There was something about him but—mmm—*something!* He seemed very interested in my chest. Ok, I am not adverse to a bit of male attention but this was very obvious. I do prefer some subtlety after all.

"Excuse me, please forgive my imposition, but I couldn't help but notice your pendant. It is quite original."

I don't often wear my gold nugget these days. My father gave it to me when I turned eighteen. It is a gold nugget from the Ballarat Goldfields and hangs around my neck on a leather cord. My father bought it on a visit to Ballarat and gave it to me at my first birthday party after I finished school. It has hung from many cords over the years and I still wear it occasionally. It always reminds me of that birthday party with my family, old school friends, and new friends from teachers' college.

"Oh, I have had it for many years, it holds rather special memories."

However there was something about the voice. People change over the years, looks change, but the voice often retains something—tone, timbre, speech patterns perhaps, and there was something about his voice.

"I once knew a girl who wore a golden nugget. Many years ago, in London."

That voice again! I was in London many years ago, more years ago than I want to admit. There was something about this man. Something familiar.

"Are you Sue Benedict?"

Oh dear. I was once Sue Benedict, after I stopped being Susan, and before I became Suzie. That was before my marriage.

"Yes." There was something familiar in the voice and the look ... not the hair, but the face and the eyes.

"I'm Peter Jamieson."

Now it all falls into place. Over thirty years ago. In England, and I left suddenly on a trip to Germany. Anywhere to get away from Peter.

"Well, this is going back a long time."

"May I join you?"

It would seem impolite to say no to his request, and it was all so long ago. So much has happened in my life since then.

"Of course, Peter. It must be at least thirty-five years since I last saw you. Do you live in Melbourne?"

"No, I'm just visiting some friends. They had some

business to attend to in the city so I came in with them, and thought I would spend some time at the Gallery while they did what they have to do. I live in Sydney now. What about you?"

"I live here. I have done for the past eight years."

"The last time I saw you, you were planning to stay in England but then you suddenly disappeared. Nobody knew where you had gone."

Well, that was not quite right. I had left London suddenly for Germany but one of my flatmates knew where I was. She was just under instructions not to tell Peter Jamieson where I had gone. She had done her job perfectly. My flatmate wrote and told me that Peter had tried to find me, but had eventually given up and left. I had never seen or heard of Peter Jamieson again. Until today.

"I had commitments in Germany, but later I returned to London. From memory you were only planning to be in London for a short time. Did you stay long in England?"

"I only stayed a month, then came back home. I spent a month travelling through South America on the way home. Then I had to settle down, get a serious job and do some work."

That was just what I had been afraid of. The last thing I had wanted to do was settle down. I had finished my teaching course, started work, saved my airfare and a little cash, and I was off to see the world. London had been fun. I had picked up casual work to pay my share of the rent, and got a few free meals at the pub where I worked. Every now and again a few of us would pool our funds, hire a van and take off somewhere. France, Italy and Germany were our favourites but we also explored Scotland and Ireland.

Life was good. Then one afternoon Peter turned up. A mutual friend had brought him along and we went out for a drink. He was great company and we soon became very good friends. A group of us used to go out together, but then it became just the two of us. Still I always knew he was only visiting and my plans were to stay for a long time. One morning I woke up and realised I had to get away from this man. That day I found a job as a nanny for an English family who were moving to Germany on business. I applied, and in three days I had gone.

Eventually I returned to London with basic German, picked up some tourist French and found a lowly job in the public relations industry through a friend. I was quite good at organising people, if I say so myself, and soon was given more responsibility. That's when I met my British husband. Well my only husband, or ex-husband to be more accurate.

"How about you? Did you stay long overseas?"

"Yes, I stayed thirty-two years. I married a Brit and only came back to Melbourne some years ago. One of my children came to Australia to visit her grandparents and to see where her mother came from. She liked it. So she got a job and stayed. Then my son joined his sister for a holiday and did the same thing. My mother was also getting quite frail, so I decided to come back to Australia. Besides I was missing the sun. Although given Melbourne weather I sometimes wonder why I chose here. I guess it is my old stomping ground and my parents were here. I went to school here, and I also did my teacher training here, so I suppose it seems like home."

"You weren't a city girl from what I remember."

"No. My parents were from the Riverina, but Melbourne

was where I went to school and then trained."

"Where are your kids now?"

"They both live in Melbourne. How about you?"

"I came home. Got a job with a mining company and dug holes. Well, really I dug minerals up and then processed them."

"Do you have a family?"

"Yes. A son."

"Are you interested in art?"

"A little. I was just wandering around the Gallery. I wanted to see the stained-glass ceiling of the Great Hall. Friends have told me about it, but it was the early Australian works I was really hoping to see. I know the Gallery has some very famous paintings. I somehow identify with them: I think it is the bush, the countryside. Unfortunately they are in a different Gallery."

"I have seen them. I love some of the paintings of that period. They are so evocative of the land and times. I guess in some way they also remind me of growing up in the Riverina. The gallery has some great works. Were you a country boy?"

"No. I was definitely a city boy, but I have spent a lot of time working in the bush. To me the mid-to-late 1800s are such a fascinating time in Australian history. So much development in the country: with the opening up of the outback, the gold rushes, and the consequent population growth. Then it all came tumbling down with the drought and the depression and the hard times that followed.

Actually, I am planning to go up to Ballarat tomorrow. I have read so much about it but have never seen it. It has such a big place in Australian history and especially in mining history. At one time it was one of the richest cities in the world."

"Sometimes, when my parents were returning from Melbourne to the sheep station, they would detour and stopover in Ballarat. My father loved the buildings and history of the place. He used to take me walking around the streets of the city and tell me stories about those early days. He loved history: Australian and ancient history. I haven't been to Ballarat in years. Actually my father bought me this gold nugget in Ballarat and gave it to me to wear as a pendant. It was my birthday present. I had my eighteenth birthday party there. I remember one other visit as well, a friend and I went up one long weekend. It was sort of a celebration when I started teaching and earning some money. We had a great time. She was almost like a sister. It does take me back."

Thinking of Ballarat and Merry brought back the memories of the last weekend Merry and I had spent together—and the mystery.

"The paintings you want to see are in the Gallery in Federation Square. It is just across the river. It is not very far. I am going there myself when I finish this coffee."

"May I come with you?"

It would seem churlish to refuse, and as we made the short walk back across the river we talked of Ballarat. Neither of us spoke of London.

As we approached Flinders Street Station, Peter pointed

out a group of angular grey and brownish buildings covered with triangular panels.

"What strange buildings."

I sensed Peter, like many others before him, was challenged by the design.

"That is Federation Square and its 'Fractal Façade'. It was very trendy when the building was constructed."

We found the Gallery entrance at the rear of the Square.

"I could use some knowledge on the Heidelberg painters. Would you be my guide?"

"Why not?" I could always come back to the Linda Jackson Exhibition another day. Besides, I hadn't seen the Australian section for years, and I always did enjoy seeing the paintings.

Together we wandered the gallery of nineteenth-century Australian art. He was certainly interested in the landscapes and the lives depicted in the paintings of the late eighteen hundreds. I could share his interest. Although the scenery was different they reminded me of my childhood growing up in the vast, open grasslands of the Riverina. Especially the famous *Shearing the Rams* by Tom Roberts. Somehow the feelings evoked by the paintings always touched me. We differed on the more modern paintings in a second room. He had little interest in the surrealist works, and, unlike me, he was not attracted by much of the Aboriginal art on display. To me the paintings were fascinating, but Peter, despite finding their stories interesting and the works often decorative, did not share my fascination. He told me that what he really wanted to see were the Bradshaw paintings in the Kimberley region of Western Australia. This style of painting had been renamed and were now called Gwion Gwion. They were a completely different style of rock art that was estimated to start around twenty to twenty-six thousand years Before Present and end around five thousand years Before Present when they were replaced by a newer, less sophisticated style of painting. There was a great deal of controversy about the art and its role in early Australian settlement. One day he hoped to go to that remote part of Australia and see the rock art in its natural setting.

The announcement came unexpectedly. Peter and I had become so involved in the paintings we hadn't realised the closing time had arrived.

"Would you care to come to Ballarat with me tomorrow? I am just going up and back in the day. I could use a good guide. I plan to catch a train out of Southern Cross Railway Station at four minutes past eight in the morning."

"I don't know, Peter. I'm not sure my knowledge is very local or up-to-date."

"I'm sure it would be most enjoyable and enlightening. We could do some sightseeing and you could tell me what you remember of the city. I promise you lunch."

I wasn't in the mood for a pick up like this. I really was not interested in a date, but the talk of Ballarat, as well as my memories of Merry and that last weekend, were still in my mind. I had enjoyed his company, and our afternoon had been interesting. I had nothing planned. Suddenly I found myself saying yes.

"Can I pick you up?"

"No, I will meet you at the station. The 8.04 train you said?"

"Can I give you a call if there are any problems?"

"I will meet you there. If I don't make it I will have had a change of mind."

I may be going to Ballarat with a man I haven't seen for over thirty-five years, but I am not giving him my phone number or an address to find me. Why? That was a question I couldn't answer—even to myself.

2 THE BALLARAT TRAIN

Peter

I arrived half an hour early at Southern Cross station, found the ticket office and bought myself a ticket. Then I found a place out of the chill breeze and morning rush of commuters and waited under the undulating steel and glass roof near the indicator showing the platform for the Ballarat train.

I was looking forward to seeing her again, but somehow I didn't really expect her to come. Although yesterday she had agreed I still half expected that she would change her mind overnight and disappear like last time. She had done that once before, and she could do it again. Then in the distance I saw her getting out of a taxi.

I felt almost a sense of relief when I saw her, and I realized how much I was looking forward to spending time with her again. She had a style and elegance that was her own. Many years ago Sue Benedict had always managed to look elegant even when wearing the bright funky clothes of London in the seventies. Unlike yesterday she was dressed in black slacks, a coffee coloured blouse and a darker brown jacket. She had a large bag over her shoulder. The high heels had gone and she was wearing flats. She was obviously dressed expecting to do some walking.

She made her way towards me, dodging through the noisy bustle of workers heading for their offices and shops, and greeted me with a formal handshake. We passed through the turnstile and found seats side by side in the leading carriage. I prefer to sit looking in the direction of travel. In fact I find it somehow unsettling to sit facing the direction from which the train has come. Side by side is not a good way to have a conversation, and I was pleased when she suggested we move to other seats and she chose a seat facing me.

After a wave from the guard and a blast on the horn the train pulled slowly away from the station. It rattled its way through the rail yards and inner city suburbs before picking up speed as it passed through the industrial area with its factories. As we reached the outskirts of the city we came to the new growth suburbs with flags proclaiming bright new residential developments. At one of these we passed a huge billboard proclaiming the features of 'Elysium Gardens', the latest development of the Grande group. I wondered how potential residents would view it, or if they would even know and think about it. Would 'Elysium Gardens' be a paradise on earth, or an abode for the dead—even if the dead were those favoured by the Gods? As so often the case the display hoarding featured happy young couples and smiling children riding bikes through pretty parks. In reality the development appeared to have small blocks and narrow streets with little parking for the three or four cars which would eventually appear as the smiling bike-riding kids grew up, found jobs, and bought cars. As yet the 'Garden' seemed to be non-existent, unless the grassed drainage channel and a few lomandras clustered around the showy entrance to the estate counted as the garden. A white truck was dumping soil or mulch near what appeared to be a children's playground. I hoped for the residents' sake that, in time, more landscaping would appear, but I was not confident of it occurring. There seemed to be some sort of gathering around a big dark car pulled up in the entrance. Even from the distance, in the brief time as the train passed, you could feel the emotion and anger of the people milling around the car.

"What do you make of that?"

Sue took a longer look out the carriage window before turning to me.

"I don't know. It looks like a dispute of some sort. Maybe a workers' strike or a community action protest. Whatever it is I get a bad feeling!"

I had to agree. The sense of tension, anger, and potential violence seemed to reach out, even into the passing train.

I had often wanted to visit Ballarat. When I commenced studying mining the goldfields of Ballarat were frequently mentioned. It was the site of the first of the economic booms that had occurred in Australia and the scene of an early move towards nationhood and separation from England.

Just as the discovery of gold in California in 1848 had started a rush with the forty-niners, the 1851 discovery of gold at Buninyong and Poverty Point started a similar rush and within a year there were twenty thousand diggers searching for gold as people flooded into the region seeking their fortunes. For some years the gold was easy to find. A few made their fortunes but, as always seems to be the case, many worked and struggled for nothing.

The flood of miners included over sixteen thousand men from China who walked overland from the colony of South

Australia to Ballarat, a distance of more than six hundred kilometres to avoid paying the Victorian tax on entering through the Port of Melbourne. By 1858 there were just under ten thousand Chinese living and working in Ballarat. Only two were women. There were two Chinese Temples established and an English-Chinese language weekly newspaper was also published.

As with so many boom towns every sort of rogue arrived to take advantage of both the wealthy and the desperate. Then when the Colonial Government in Melbourne sought to tax the miners at higher and higher rates an armed rebellion broke out and the miners erected a defensive stockade. The military were called to put down the uprising. The miners, who were poorly prepared for rebellion, included a mounted group of two hundred Americans calling themselves 'The Independent Californian Rangers'. Most of this group were away from the stockade attempting to prevent the arrival of government reinforcements reaching Ballarat when the battle broke out. The battle only lasted around fifteen minutes but it led to the government of the colony of Victoria changing the laws and abolishing the expensive gold miner's licence fee, replacing it with a much cheaper Miner's Right, and giving miners political representation in the government. The leader of the uprising even went on to eventually become the Speaker of the Legislative Assembly for Victoria.

The memories of those days still linger in the Eureka flag and the grand bank buildings that appeared along Lydiard Street.

The incredible wealth flowing into Ballarat and Melbourne had caused a huge building boom which in turn attracted even more speculative funds. Melbourne became one of the richest and grandest cities in the world. In the British Empire it was second only to London in size. However, by then, the gold was becoming harder to find and more expensive to mine. The attention shifted to the Rand in Africa which had its turn for a gold boom in 1886. As so often happens, the craziness of the boom times ended for Ballarat and Melbourne with the crash of 1891.

What particularly interested me was the change in mining as it moved from alluvial mining to deep underground mining with shafts and cages and underground leads. The techniques, equipment and investment needed were familiar to me.

As the train passed Ballan I asked Sue if she knew Ballarat very well.

"Please call me Suzie. Nobody has called me Sue for so many years. My parents used to call me Susan but eventually even they changed."

She told me her father had managed a large sheep station in the Riverina for an English company. The board of Directors in London rarely visited and he had free rein to manage it as he saw fit. The years were good and when he retired the company very generously gave him a trip to England as a retirement bonus. Rather than be educated at home by her mother or a governess, Sue, Suzie, was sent to school in Melbourne.

Occasionally when she was coming home from boarding school the family would make a detour and break the journey. They would stay overnight in Ballarat, and do some sightseeing. Her father had always enjoyed the history of the area, the beautiful old buildings and particularly the parks and gardens around Lake Wendouree.

"I remember when I was quite small my father reminded me to be very careful about the Ballarat trams. He had a friend whose father had been accidently run over by one and killed."

For her eighteenth birthday the family had made it the site for her birthday party. It was central and more convenient for her friends from the Riverina and Western districts as well as Melbourne to attend.

Some years later she had spent a long weekend revisiting the city with a friend. She had commenced boarding school the same day as Mary and they had immediately become firm friends. The friendship had continued throughout their school years and they had often spent holidays visiting each other's family. Since she was an only child, Mary became the sister that Suzie would have loved to have had.

Mary was working as a secretary in a big legal firm in Melbourne and when Suzie finished her teacher training and started work they decided to celebrate their new financial freedom with a long weekend away. Ballarat was the choice. Like us they had taken the train from Southern Cross, although in those days it was known as Spencer St. Station.

Suzie stopped speaking and looked out the window. It was as if some other thought had taken hold of her mind and she did not wish to talk about it. A sadness came into her eyes.

Suzie

The conversation had stalled. My mind had drifted back to that previous visit with Merry. I stopped speaking. Peter did not break my silence but looked out the window and left me with my thoughts. Finally I gathered my senses and returned to the present.

"My friend's name was Merry, like Merry Christmas, not the usual 'a r y'. She was christened Meredith Elizabeth Oliver. Her mother's name was Meredith and the family planned to call her Elizabeth, however she was such a happy smiling baby they used to call her Merry Elizabeth. The name suited her and she became just Merry. At school she was officially Meredith Elizabeth but all the teachers called her Merry. The girls shortened it again and we often called her Meres. The name just suited her."

Again I drifted into silence thinking about her. When I returned to the present for the second time I decided I really should find out more about this man who I had once known and was now sitting opposite me. So much has happened in my life since I first met him, his life must have many mysteries as well.

"Do you often come to Melbourne?"

"No, not that often. These days most of my time is in Sydney. We have a lovely house out on Pittwater. It is part of Sydney but when you are there the city seems far away."

"Are you married?"

"I was, but my wife died four years ago."

"I'm sorry. Were you married for very long?"

"Yes, Claire and I were married for thirty six years. She was a very special woman. Our friends described her as a sparkling jewel with a rock. I was the rock."

I smiled. I could see Peter as a rock. He seemed so solid and reliable. Not like my ex! I had sometimes felt like throwing rocks at him. Eventually we had reached a workable understanding but my description of him in those strained days was more turd than rock. Nor had I ever been thought of as a sparkling jewel by him. Tony had called me many things I mostly preferred to forget. He used to refer to me as the 'Ice Maiden' among his friends. How quickly our ideas can change, that had not been his idea when we first married. Perhaps it became true as our relationship deteriorated.

"What was she like?"

"Claire liked people and she loved nature. She always looked for the good things in life. Sometimes it worried me that she didn't see the dark side that can exist under the surface. But then, that may be a great way to live—if you only see the good in people."

"How did you meet her?"

"After I came back from London I got a job in a copper mine in Cobar. That was quite a change from London! I needed a proper job and some money. When I had finished my mining engineering degree at Uni I got a job in a mine and saved up enough cash for a few months travel and that was when I met you in London. There was not a lot of work for a hard rock miner in London, and I didn't want to do the usual bar work or labouring that so many Aussies did on their overseas experience. My parents weren't flush with funds after helping me through Uni and I needed to get started on a career. I did still want to see other parts of the world, and when I saw a job offer to work for a copper mine in Zambia I took it and left Cobar. When we had time off some of us used to fly down to Cape Town for a break. That's where I met Claire."

"She was South African?"

"No, Australian. She had travelled in an expedition truck from London to Cape Town. She was back-packing in Cape Town when I met her. We met up a few times in South Africa until she returned to Australia and then when I came back here I looked her up. The rest is history. Last year I was in Namibia working on a project and I saw an expedition truck full of young people doing the same trek. It bought back so many memories."

"Did you continue to work in mining?"

"Yes. For years we moved from mine camp to mine camp. In those days the mines provided staff accommodation for management. Eventually we decided that we needed a permanent base to provide an education for our son so then I would spend time on site and accumulate days to spend at home with Claire. Really I think Claire mostly raised our son. She had to deal with the scrapes and scratches and the broken arm. Then she had the teenage years! At least she could finally have a garden. She loved plants and for years she had had to make do with pots, and quite often with insufficient water supplies. She could finally indulge her love for native plants and develop a garden."

I love gardening. It is one of my pleasures to work in the garden of my home in Melbourne but I am a rose and perennials person. I love the look of English cottage gardens; natives are not my thing.

"Are you still working?"

"I still do a little work as a consultant. My speciality is

hard rock. I was doing a report for an English company with interests in copper mines in Namibia. I knew the manager. He is Australian."

"What does your son do?"

"Matthew is in mining like me. Well more oil and gas. He has a job on the North West Shelf. These days he is based in Karratha."

"What about grandchildren?"

"No. Matthew doesn't seem interested in even having a permanent partner—so no grandchildren. I think that was Claire's, and my, hope but it was not to be. You don't have an available daughter do you?"

As a matter of fact I do. Emma also seems to have no interest in a permanent partner. There have been a number of men in her life but none stay for too long. I sometimes wondered whether my broken marriage has affected the way she sees relationships. She tells me no, she is just waiting for Mr Right but like so many girls her age I think she has set unrealistic expectations of Mr Right. Perhaps Mr Right wouldn't see her as Mrs Right. She would probably demand to be Ms Right. She is very forthright and strong-willed. I tried to imagine her on an oil rig off the coast of Western Australia. It would be so far away from the inner city coffee shops and cultural events of the big cities she loves.

"Yes I do, but she is very much an inner city girl. I don't see her on an oil rig. She would probably be more likely to be protesting about ruining the environment."

Emma is usually concerned about some issue or other, however most of her protests seem to be done over cups of coffee or glasses of wine with her friends, or in writing letters to like-minded magazines. I share many of her concerns but not with the passion she has. Sometimes I think she is too narrow-minded in her outlook and fails to see the ramifications of her ideas. I worry that she is so concerned with 'saving' and 'stopping' that she never considers how to provide positive answers to the world's problems.

"She's not a lesbian?" Peter's blunt enquiry surprised me. I could see Emma loudly supporting an individual's rights to their sexual preferences but I suspected deep down she didn't approve. She certainly showed no sign of it in her own life. Peter continued.

"I had an aunt, well she was actually a great aunt. It was many years ago. She shared a house with another woman. My aunt was an English rose and her friend was a very severe woman who wore lace up men's shoes and dark suits. They bickered like an old married couple and as a young lad I used to wonder about them. The family never discussed their relationship. I have no idea what their arrangement was but it was certainly emotional."

"You've asked about my daughter. What about your son? There's a lot of it about these days?"

"I did wonder but I don't think so. I think he is just one of those old fashioned bachelors that never marry. He is a great honorary 'uncle'. I've seen him with his friend's kids and they love him. He would make a great father. These days there are more women working in the mines and the gas industry but they are still scarce. I wish he would find a good woman and get married. The companionship when you get older is precious."

His remark jolted me. Don't tell me Peter is a sad old man looking for company in his dotage. The last thing I want in my life is to be the carer of an old man. I have my friends and family. I don't need that. He doesn't really seem to be sad, actually it is interesting to be with him and he is good company. He doesn't look like he is in his dotage either. If he is I must be getting close because I am sure he is only a few years older than me. Sometimes it would be nice to come home to a welcoming hug and a warm house. It is so long since that has happened and I have put it out of my life.

"Well that's my life story. What about yours?"

"You heard most of it yesterday. Not much to say. I stayed in England, got married, had two children, got divorced, and eventually came back to Australia. The kids had already come out here and settled. My parents were here, although they have both since died. I have made my life here now."

"You don't miss life in England?"

"Some things, some friends, but really the kids and my grandson are here. They are the most important people in my life. I don't miss UK weather. Even Melbourne is much better."

There was a lot more I could tell Peter but I was not going to open my life to someone I had just met, even if we had been close years ago.

"Some years ago, before she became sick, Claire and I did a trip to Europe and the UK. She wanted to show me the places she had seen when she was travelling. This time it was in tour buses, not some ageing Kombi. That, and apart from one month in Britain, and most of that was in London, as you know, my travels have been to out of the way mine sites—not castles and cathedrals."

As the train continued aged hedges of broken cypresses

began to appear. The attempt by early settlers to create a touch of England thwarted by the twisted gums and their scraggly branches still standing along roadways and in paddocks. As we approached Ballarat some deciduous trees were just starting to turn.

"Do you have any suggestions as to what we should do?"

"Peter, it is so long since I was last here. I'm sure it has all changed. I remember the railway station is in the centre of town and quite close to the main street which had some beautiful buildings. Perhaps we could just walk and keep our eyes open for a tourist information centre. I imagine there will be one somewhere."

"For a miner like me Sovereign Hill could be interesting. It is an open air museum of gold mining and a re-creation of early Ballarat. Probably not so much for the mining technology but more for the way of life in those days. However I think it really needs more time to visit than we have. It could be a place to take your grandson someday."

Peter's interest in Ballarat's history was obvious and he had certainly done his research. I supposed it was the mining boom that had caught his imagination. As we walked from the train station and started down Lydiard Street he pointed out the grand Victorian era bank buildings and hotels that gold had financed. Banks, with once well-known names which had disappeared in mergers, or worse, in failures, were now solicitor's or accountant's offices. Hotels which had survived by re-inventing themselves to the times. Here and there more modern buildings had inserted themselves into the streetscape, their shop fronts so different to the staid old banks. Further down the street we came to the beautiful wrought iron veranda of the Mining Exchange.

Peter explained it was once home to share brokers and agents selling shares in mines. When it opened in the late 1880s it had almost one hundred members. Then the decline started.

Crossing Sturt Street we came to Her Majesty's Theatre. I remembered the building was the home of the famous South Street Eisteddfod. What I hadn't realised was that it was constructed over a mineshaft. When it was built in 1875 it was called The Academy of Music. The other theatres of the day were considered as being far too risqué for polite society.

Peter's homework of internet searches and reading made the walk with him fascinating. He was a great tourist guide.

"Do you know Dame Nellie Melba sang here? And over there is the hotel, the one with the tower, where she stayed. Let's have lunch there. I saw on the Internet they have a wonderful old bar and a very lovely dining room."

There was one special place nearby that Peter wanted to see. He told me the story of the fighting that took place under the corner of Dana Street and Lydiard Street South. When one mining company's tunnel broke into a rival's tunnel underground warfare erupted with stink bombs of burning sulphur hurled into each other's tunnels.

"I read about that event when I was a child. It has always fascinated me. Ever since then I have wanted to stand over the very spot. Now I have done it. I've fulfilled a childhood dream."

Further on we found the old goal, dating from the days of the early gold rush, now part of the University. We returned to our chosen lunch spot. The hotel had started life in 1853 as a timber building but had quickly been rebuilt as a far grander hotel in 1857. As the wealth of the city grew the hotel was extended in 1890 and '91. The old cedar work and decor had been lovingly restored in period style. What had once been part of the hotel yard was now a bright airy conservatory. We were shown to a table looking out into a small courtyard with a gently splashing fountain.

"When we came into the hotel did you see the board mounted on the wall showing some of the hotel's history? The Royal commission into the Eureka Stockade was held on this site. Nellie Melba sang from the balcony of the hotel and Mark Twain stayed here. There was quite a list of important personages mentioned including British royalty and the captain of an American Confederate Naval ship visiting the colony of Victoria."

The food was not period style. The menu was modern. I decided on a small serve of pasta and clams with garlic and chilli. Peter looked over the menu and ordered a small steak. Then he ordered an entrée of pork belly and black pudding saying he really liked pork belly. I wondered what Emma would say to him. Her taste in food these days was vegetarian. She was still trying to convince me to give up meat. Having grown up on a sheep station that was not going to happen! I had once tried to explain to her that not all country was suitable for growing food crops, and perhaps we should eat animals that could convert rough grasses into meat that humans could eat. To not utilise those rangelands would be to deprive the world of a valuable food source. In reply I got, "Mother!" I was obviously irredeemable.

With our meal finished, Peter was ready to continue the tour.

"Let's go back down the hill and walk Sturt Street."

"Left or right?"

"Let's go left. It looks more interesting."

Peter and I wandered along the wide avenue admiring the buildings and statues. Standing in front of the statues of Hebe and Ruth I looked across the street and saw it. The memories came rushing back, and this time they had a sense of dread!

3 MERRY'S STORY

Suzie

"I remember that hotel!

It is where Merry and I stayed when we came to Ballarat the last weekend I saw her. Merry had booked the hotel. She had heard her brother, Billy, talking about how smart it was, but when she told him we were planning to stay there he became quite angry and told her emphatically not to stay there. When she told him she had already booked, and she would not change her plans, he was very annoyed. I think Merry wanted to see what it was like. Let's go inside."

The hotel was no longer the smart hotel I remembered from our stay. Like the British Empire, the Grand Imperial had seen better days. Nor was it any longer grand. The reception desk was unattended and the hotel looked as if it had hardly been maintained for many years. The paint on the walls was faded, the carpet aged and worn. The furniture I remembered as modern and fashionable on my visit with Merry now looked dated. Where once the hotel had had a consistency of style, obviously from some interior designer's input, now it was a hodgepodge of cheap additions from the eighties and more recent years. They neither matched nor complimented the original tables and chairs that remained from the earlier grander times. Its smart days had ended many years earlier and it now must survive, if it could be called survival, on serious drinkers. We found the bar off to the side and waited for a barman to come. The poker machines were unattended by patrons. We were the only clients.

Peter bought a glass of white wine for me, and a beer for himself, and we sat at a table and surveyed the hotel.

"That weekend was a long weekend. I went into the city and met Merry after she finished work. We caught the train to Ballarat. Back then the hotel was very smart and shiny. Very modern. Flash comes to mind. We checked in and decided to try the bar. As I remember it called itself the 'Sportsman's Bar'. There were photos of racehorses, cricket teams and the usual sporting odds and sods. There were people around the bar after work. Then we went into the dining room. It had some fancy name and the latest fashionable food, probably prawn cocktails! After dinner we decided to go back to the bar to see what was happening. We were two girls on a night out!

By then the crowd had changed. There were only a few men at the bar and some women sitting together around a table. Occasionally a man would come in, chat to them, and one would go with him in the lift."

"You think it was her husband?"

"Well someone's husband. Merry and I thought we might be able to pick up some business if we had wanted to—but we weren't dressed appropriately!"

"How do you mean?"

"Not enough makeup and no high heels."

"Do you think it was a brothel?"

"No, I don't think so, but there was something strange about it, and there seemed to be lots of people, men and women, coming into the hotel. They would see the desk clerk and go to the lift. Others just went straight to the lift. I guess they had their keys. Yet next morning there appeared to be very few people staying in the hotel. We noticed the lift indicator also seemed to be unreliable. Sometimes the indicator lights would show which floor they went to and other times it didn't work. I remember now. Merry said she had heard a rumour at work that it was an illegal gambling house.

We spent three nights here and we didn't really feel comfortable. The place just made us uneasy. By Sunday we started to avoid the lounge and go straight to our room. We just had a bad feeling.

Let's leave! Thinking about that weekend and Merry has brought back memories and this place still has a bad vibe. I feel very close to her."

On the trip back to Melbourne I told Peter the story of Merry.

"We had been best friends at school and remained so after we had left school. We had shared a flat together with two other girls while I was doing my teacher's training. Merry had finished her secretarial course and picked up a job working for the father of another of her friends in his legal office in the city. My first teaching job was in the country but I used to crash on the floor if there was a party or some other reason to be in Melbourne. We used to have great fun and lots of laughs.

One day she disappeared. She finished work and was never seen again. The other girls in the flat weren't too concerned when she didn't arrive home. They assumed that she might have stayed in the city for drinks or dinner. Next morning when she still wasn't home they really became worried. It was so unlike her. If she was staying out she would usually let one of them know. By the afternoon they still hadn't heard from her so they started ringing around her friends. No one knew anything of her. They then tried to phone her parents but couldn't contact them. That's when they contacted the police. The police investigated, checked out her friends and work associates but no one had any information. She had walked out of the office at the usual time and just disappeared. No one has heard anything of her since that day."

"Do you think she ran off with someone?"

"No, I knew her as well as anyone, probably better. She was like a sister. We shared each other's secrets. She had some boyfriends but no one in particular and she showed no interest in a serious relationship."

"Maybe there was a jealous lover?"

"The police checked out all her male friends. They were cleared. There was no sign of a stalker."

"Do you think she might have been kidnapped?"

"What for? Melbourne in those days was hardly the home of the white slave trade. Besides, the police had made enquiries and there was no indication of that happening at the time. It is still a mystery. What made it worse for her family is that the day following her disappearance her brother was killed in a car crash. So not only did they have to cope with Merry's disappearance but also Billy's death."

Thinking of Merry had brought back so many old memories. I remembered our times at school and our holidays at her home in the Western District. I was very fond of her parents and had kept in touch with them even when I was in England. Her father had died but her mother and sister still lived on the property near Penshurst. It was years since I had last seen them. I decided I wanted to see them again.

"Would you like a drive down to the Western District? I want to go and see Merry's mother. This trip has brought all the memories back and I was very fond of her. Perhaps, if Meredith is home, we could drive down on Thursday and see her."

"I still have a week before I'm booked to fly back to Sydney, and my friends are working during the week so they won't be worried. Yes, that would be good."

When the train pulled into Southern Cross station we parted. I found a taxi and Peter went looking for a train to take him to his friend's home. I'd arranged to pick him up near the station, at eight thirty Thursday morning, for an overnight stay with the Olivers. Then I realised I didn't even have his phone number or know where he was living. I hadn't contacted the Olivers and yet for some reason I had invited him to visit one of my oldest and dearest friends.

4 OAKLEIGH

Suzie

Peter was waiting for me at our agreed pickup point near the station. I unlocked the car door and he got in. Melbourne was doing its 'four seasons in one day' weather, and with the traffic and occasional scuds of rain Peter sensed I didn't want to talk. By the time we got to Inverleigh the rain had cleared completely and the sun came out as we drove past the old drystone fences of early sheep runs. We pulled over to the side of the road near a cypress windbreak for a coffee from the flask I had brought with me. Reaching Mortlake we stopped, found a pie shop and bought pies and another coffee. I didn't want to arrive at Oakleigh at meal time.

Forty-five minutes brought us to the turn-off to the Oakleigh road. A few minutes more and we were at the bluestone entrance to Oakleigh with its massive pillars and old wrought iron gates. As I drove through the gates and down the century old drive of cypress trees all the memories came rushing back to me. I had spent many school holidays here with Merry. We had met on our first day at boarding school. Two little girls far from our homes and both on our own. Our friendship had grown until she became the sister I had never had.

When I came to Oakleigh on school holidays it had been continual fun, swimming in the lake, tennis afternoons, woolshed dances and parties. Together we had discovered boys and spent many hours in hushed conference together.

Life on the land had been so different then. It was after the Korean War. That war had been in a cold climate and the demand for wool had risen dramatically causing the prices to rise as well. The wool industry boomed and money flowed into the bush. It was the time of 'a pound a pound'; a pound of wool was worth one Australian pound of money. Prices that had never been seen again in the wool industry, especially as the pound changed to dollars, and then kilograms replaced the pound for weight. Costs were also much lower, and for some to grow wool was to have undreamed of wealth. Even though incomes had fallen by the time Merry and I met at school, money was still plentiful from those bountiful years.

As we approached the homestead a dirt road went off to the left. I remembered it. It led to the back door of the homestead and to the staff houses and workshops. From there it went on to the woolshed and sheep yards. I toyed with the idea of going to the backdoor as country people usually did, but when I had phoned Meredith Oliver she had mentioned that the garden driveway had just been re-gravelled and to drive carefully so I decided we should use the formal entrance. Smaller bluestone posts flanked the stock grid as we drove into the garden. The old trees in the garden looked the same but gone were the beds of annuals that Mrs Oliver so loved. Now the garden was stripped back to make it easier to manage and the walks allowed to grass over. The gardeners that once worked on so many stations had long gone.

Merry's sister met us at the porte cochere. Jane was Merry's older sister by seven years. When we were at school she had seemed so sophisticated. Merry had been a bridesmaid at her wedding and I remembered how grown up and beautiful Merry had looked in her bridesmaid dress. It was such a change from our daggy school uniforms. Then Jane had moved away with her husband and soon had a baby boy. Now she had returned to Oakleigh to be with her mother. The only child left of the family.

"Welcome back to Oakleigh. It is so long since we have seen you. Mother is inside, she wants to see you. Edward, my son, will be in later. He is out in the paddocks checking some stock."

"Hello Susan. It is so good to see you again."

"Thank you for having us, Mrs Oliver. It brings back so many memories coming here."

"Yes, you and Merry were such good friends and you were always so much fun, even when you were a little naughty."

The sadness in her eyes increased with her memories of those days.

"What brings you back?"

I explained Peter's and my interest in the mystery of Merry's disappearance and the old hotel and how we felt there must be a clue somewhere, perhaps here.

"I don't know how. It was all so long ago. So much has changed."

Meredith Oliver was no longer the lively blonde lady I remembered from schooldays. Then she had always seemed happy and smiling with a home that was welcoming and warm. Now she was an old lady, grey-haired, but still very correct. She must be in her nineties I thought. When I first met her she would have been in her early forties. Her once lively eyes now held a sadness that had not been there before Merry vanished and Billy was killed.

Later Peter and I went for a walk in the garden. It was full of memories. The elms Merry and I climbed as kids, the hawthorn hedge we hid behind and the old horse chestnut. Even the century old oak tree where I had my first kiss. How Merry and I giggled over that in our bedroom that night.

"I remember this elm. Look, there's the hook. There used to be a swinging cane basket chair hanging from it. Merry and I used to spend hours crammed in it together talking about what we would do when we finished school. She didn't get time to do much of it. She disappeared three years after we left school."

"What about you?"

"Oh I did some of it, but then ... Let's not go there."

Peter's question had not just brought more memories of Merry to mind but also thoughts of my own life. I was grateful when a twin cab drove up and a man got out.

"Hello. I'm Edward, you must be Susan and Peter. Mother called on the radio to say if I passed you to let you know dinner is just about ready. Do you want a lift?"

The last time I saw Edward he was a toddler. Now he was

a grown man, suddenly I felt my age. With Peter I felt young.

"Thank you but we will walk back. We were just discussing how your aunt and I used to sit in a swing here."

"We took that down years ago. It became unsafe and we were afraid it would break. I used to try to make it swing up as high as possible, and Mum and Dad thought I would kill myself so they took it down."

"Your aunt and I used to sit here for hours talking. Do you remember your aunt?"

"Not really. I was only four when she died. I guess any memory I have comes from what my parents have told me."

"You said she died."

"Well she must have. That's the way they talk. It's the same as with Uncle Bill."

After dinner Peter went to the kitchen to help Jane tidy the plates and dishes from the evening meal. I sat with Mrs Oliver in the formal lounge. Unlike some of the other rooms in the house it had hardly changed from all those years ago, except for a few new photos and a coat of paint, the same colour as I remembered from the past. Only Mrs Oliver was different and the feeling of the room had lost its vitality.

"I had to come and see Oakleigh again," I explained. "I hope you don't mind. The thought of Merry just became so insistent I had to come back."

"It seems so long ago and yet I live with it every day. I'm not sure which is worse, to know your son is dead or to not know what happened to your daughter. Colin and I were always thinking of her, but since his death—well, now it's just me."

"It must have been doubly painful to lose your son and then find out Merry was missing."

"The night we got the phone call that Billy's car had crashed was terrible. We raced to the hospital but by the time we got there he was already dead."

"Where was he going?"

"He never said. He got a phone call and he said he would have to leave immediately. Some friend I think, although we never found out who it was. Billy seemed very agitated and worried and left straight away even though it was raining heavily and getting dark. He wouldn't wait until the morning, saying he had to go at once. We thought he was going to Melbourne. He had been moody all that week. It was so unlike him. He was usually the life of the party. In fact Colin and I used to worry he was a bit irresponsible."

"What happened?"

"He hit a tree on the road near Scarsdale. The doctor said it would have been immediate. We hope he didn't suffer."

"What day was that?"

"July 17, it was a Saturday."

That was one day after Merry had left work and disappeared.

"We tried to contact Merry about her brother but there was no answer at her flat. We went to the hospital, the ambulance had taken him into Ballarat, and then went on to Melbourne to Merry's flat but she wasn't there and her flatmates said they hadn't seen her for two days. They had become worried and had tried to phone us but of course we were on the road. There were no mobile phones in those days. They had phoned all her friends but no one knew where she was. Eventually they called the police. When we arrived in Melbourne and found she was missing we called all our friends to ask if anyone had seen her. No one had. We even thought she may have gone up to your parents' in the Riverina, but no one knew anything. It was just so unlike her. The police tried but they could find no trace of her. She left work one night and nobody ever saw her again."

I remembered the calls from the worried parents as they became more and more frantic as the days passed without any news.

"What do you think happened?"

"I don't know, it was so unlike her. Some people say she must have had a boyfriend and ran off with him, but that wasn't her. She was always so open".

I thought of some of our conversations in the swing chair. Perhaps her mother didn't always know the full story but I couldn't see Merry running off with some new love. It just wasn't her.

Walking down the hallway with Peter towards our separate bedrooms I had flashbacks of the times Merry and I had taken late night walks in the garden—and of our secret midnight confessions. I felt a sudden desire to walk in the garden again. I asked Peter if he would join me. The sunshine and warmth of the afternoon had made way for one of those cooler breezes that can make the late summer nights so beautiful, and the almost full moon in the cloudless night sky lit our walk. The scent from the night jasmine drifted across our pathway. Was it just the night, or me, but I felt an unaccustomed stirring I had not felt for many years. We strolled across the lawn and down to the lake without saying a word, just enjoying the coolness, the breeze in the trees, the sounds of the crickets and the moonlight. In the distance the twin volcanic cones of Mount Rouse were still just visible beyond the lake. I felt an urge to reach out to Peter but I couldn't. What a silly idea!

Then Peter's voice broke into my thoughts.

"After dinner, when you were in the lounge with Meredith, I was talking with Jane in the kitchen. I asked about her brother. She was very protective but there seems to be something else. Do you know what it might have been?"

"Perhaps it concerns the car crash. Billy was a bit of a playboy. Well, he liked the high life, parties, racing and booze. Some of the boys got carried away with the easy money and didn't adjust when it stopped. Merry adored him, and was very protective of him, but I don't think she approved of some of his friends, or the fact that he had neglected his farm management course. If there were picnic races, or any race meeting for that matter, he was off. I think it worried his parents too. He was going to Melbourne to see a friend the night he died."

"I know what you mean. You probably didn't have them at teacher's college, but I saw some of that type at university. Even after the wool boom ended they kept spending, then selling land until the back paddock became the front yard. It was often too many parties, too many race horses and too much booze."

"You are sounding like a real wowser."

"Suzie, I'm not! But it happened, and I didn't approve. You do have responsibilities."

"And what about you, I don't remember you as very responsible in London."

"I wasn't that bad!"

"You did enjoy a party if I remember."

"Well especially if you were there. I wonder who Billy was going to see in Melbourne."

"Peter, are you changing the subject?"

"Do you really know he was going to Melbourne? That was just speculation. Perhaps he was going somewhere else but obviously didn't get there. Just the way Jane spoke I wondered if there was more to the crash than they say. Could it have been deliberate?"

"You mean suicide. No. There was some talk but no one thought it likely. There seemed to be no reason. Although he had become moody—which was not his usual nature. I think Merry knew something but would never talk about it. Perhaps she didn't really know, although they were very close. He was very fond of his little sister."

"What about girls. Could he have been visiting someone? He would not have been the first man to get an urgent call from a girlfriend with a problem, 'something's late; I'm pregnant'."

"Are you speaking from experience?"

"I have seen it."

"I don't know. We had mutual friends, well more acquaintances. He was only one year older than Merry so we often went to the same places. Actually he also had other friends but we didn't see them much. I don't think Merry approved of them. I know she refused a few dates from some of Billy's friends."

"So there could have been a woman, or a man?"

"I don't think a man is likely. He seemed to date lots of female friends but never seriously. I don't recall any dark mysterious man or woman attending his funeral."

Walking back to the house we both fell silent. When we reached the hallway we hesitated. The photos of earlier Olivers watched from the walls as we turned to our rooms.

Next morning I asked Mrs Oliver and Jane if I could show Peter the old woolshed. In its early days Oakleigh had been the woolshed section of a much larger station. Over the years these huge old stations or runs had been broken up into smaller and smaller parcels of land. The Oakleigh block was still substantial by modern standards but only a small portion of what the shed had originally been built to service. Even the large old Oakleigh homestead was originally only the manager's house. The owner's house of those earlier days was miles away and much grander.

The shed had been built of bluestone and stood as testament to the workmanship of the men who had constructed it. It had been built in 1869 in an earlier wool boom and once had twenty-eight stands for shearers. Nowadays the Olivers were only using four. The yards outside had been paved with stones when it was built and some still remained in a few yards. Aged pepperina trees shaded the northern side of the yards and rows of cypresses acted as a windbreak protecting the yards and shed from the southerly and westerly winds.

I love the smell of woolsheds and the patterns the timber pens and slatted floors make. The smell of lanolin from the wool that had worked its way into the timber over a hundred years or more always affected me and brought back childhood memories. At home, when I was growing up, it had been a special treat to visit the woolshed at shearing time. In those days women were not allowed into the woolsheds. My father would always check with the shearers to see if they would agree, and then my mother and I could visit and watch them working. When the shearers had left I would go and lie in the bins of soft, white fleeces and feel the fleeces envelop me. Today women are a big part of the shearing team, some are even shearers. That would have been unimaginable in my father's time.

Relegated to a corner stood the huge old wooden Humble and Sons wool press, replaced by a modern hydraulic press that worked with the flick of a switch rather than the man powered wire cables and winches of the past.

Later Edward took Peter and me for a drive around the property. For me it was like visiting my past. I had visited the Olivers after Merry's disappearance but then I had left for England. Although we kept in touch I had only once visited since my return and that had been a brief stay. Driving around looking at the sheep I realised the changes that had taken place. Once there would have been wool breeds of sheep but now the price of wool was low and the market was for meat sheep. The whole industry had changed from what I remembered from my youth. Peter was ever the gentleman opening and shutting gates as we drove through them while Edward and I talked and talked of the past and the present. I realised how much of my country upbringing I missed.

Back at the homestead Peter and I took another walk in the garden.

"How long have the Olivers lived here?"

"I don't really know. I remember, when we were a school, Merry saying that they had been here for many years. I think she said the family had first bought the property when Victoria was still a colony. That would have been before federation in 1901. I remember meeting her grandparents once. They had worked Oakleigh and gone through good years and bad. I think they may have had more bad years than good. I remember hearing stories of the damage that bushfires had done to properties and of course there were the inevitable droughts."

"What about Billy? What was he like?"

"He was a year older than Merry but had quite a different personality. When he left school he came home and worked on Oakleigh before he went off to Agricultural College to learn property management. I gather it didn't work the way it should have and he was sent off as a jackaroo to a sheep stud in the west of New South Wales. That was like doing an apprenticeship in the pastoral industry. Jackaroos weren't paid much and had to work hard, but they could get good training if they worked for the right person. Good jackaroos then worked their way up to management positions. That's what my father did. Jackaroos were also expected to have some social graces. The wool industry in those days could be very snobby. Getting a position at some big studs required going to the right private school and having the best social contacts. After two years Billy came back and worked here. I expect the Olivers wanted him to be more involved in running Oakleigh."

"What was he like as a person?"

"I don't think he took responsibility very seriously. Meres loved a party but it never interfered with her work. I don't think Billy had the same attitude. He was very popular and had lots of friends who seemed to prefer parties to work. I suppose, in time, they would have grown up."

"What about Merry?"

"As I said she loved a party. She was an outgoing personality and one of those people who loved life and people, but she was also responsible. I think she was popular at work. It was always fun to be around her. She wasn't perfect. She could be very impetuous. Meres just did things and she wasn't always on time. That sometimes annoyed me. At school I was called 'Little Miss Organised'."

As I said it I thought, I've just gone on a day trip to Ballarat with a man I haven't seen for forty years and then I invite him to meet the mother of my oldest friend. That is just not like me!

"Merry was also very loyal. One girl at school had parents who were going through some very public and messy business. Many of the girls shunned her. Merry was her friend and she never changed her attitude. She stuck with her when everyone else was giving the poor girl a hard time. If anything Merry would rush in without any regard for the consequences. Occasionally I would have to rescue her."

"Last night when you were talking to Meredith and I was in the kitchen with Jane, she also mentioned that she had once overheard a disagreement between her parents and

Billy. Apparently Jane had come on a visit and her parents hadn't realised she had arrived. It seems the local SP bookie had approached her father at a sheep sale about some debt Billy had run up with him. Her father was furious and demanding a promise that he wouldn't gamble anymore. When she entered the room the conversation stopped. She never heard any more about the subject."

"I know he loved going to the races with his mates. It would not have surprised me if he punted. Many of his mates used to boast about their bets but I don't know about Billy. I never heard him talk about winning or losing. Perhaps we should go back to the house. They must be wondering where we have gone."

5 DRIVING BACK TO MELBOURNE

Suzie

After breakfast we took our leave of the Olivers and started our drive back to Melbourne. The morning was sunny and the sky cloudless. One of those March days which are neither too hot nor too cold and without the cold wind that sometimes blows across the Western district. I was driving with Peter in the passenger seat. Men might have mid-life crises but women have menopause. If a man wants to buy a red sports car and get a new trophy wife then I can buy my own convertible.

This was the first car that was ever really mine. I have had many cars over the years. My husband believed in changing cars every three years and although some were supposed to be 'your car', I always seemed to end up with the car he wanted for me, not the one I would have bought for myself. Even my old second-hand VW 'Bertie' that I loved for years, and sat in a shed and waited when I was overseas, wasn't really my choice as my Dad had chosen it for me and paid for it when I left school. This one was really mine. I picked the car, I picked the colour and I paid for it.

I loved the colour, a bright yellow the manufacturer called 'Sunburst' or something creative. I preferred to think of it as Sunshine Yellow or Sunflower Yellow. It always seemed such a happy colour. I loved my SLK 320 convertible. And there was no way a man was going to drive my car.

"This isn't the way we came from Melbourne."

"No, we went the direct way by the Hamilton highway. This is more scenic."

I had decided to return by the Great Ocean Road. It was a longer, slower way to Melbourne but it was a beautiful day and the road along the coast is one of the great scenic drives of the world. The first part of the trip down to Warrnambool was through farming country, then we turned east onto the Great Ocean Road. The scenic drive runs for two hundred and forty-nine kilometres from Warrnambool to Torquay. It had been commenced as an employment program for soldiers returning from the Great War of 1914–1918. Using only picks and shovels they had built the road along the coast as a Memorial to those who had not returned. In parts the winding road runs along headlands and cliffs, or cuts through tall forests and heathlands. In other places it crosses river floodplains and runs alongside beaches.

We pulled into a car park and took the walking track through the heath to the lookout where I showed Peter the famous view of the Twelve Apostles. He told me he had never been to this part of Australia before, most of his travels and work had been in the north or west. Back in the car and sheltering from the coastal wind I poured coffees.

As we approached Apollo Bay neither of us had spoken for quite a while so I turned on the radio. As usual my radio was tuned to Radio National.

"Do you listen to that station?"

"Yes, of course, they usually have interesting programs."

"Oh well."

It was obvious that Peter was not a fan.

"What's the problem?"

"They always seem to have some problem. It's always land rights, the environment, global warming, racism, sexism and women issues."

One of my dearest friends from my childhood in the country claimed the radio station was always promoting 'Land rights for Lesbian Whales'. I had to agree with him. The station was always having programs on land rights for aborigines, or programs about the environment, or minority sexual preferences. The discussions always appeared to be very one-sided. These days he would probably have added global warming to the list.

"Do you have a problem with those things?"

"Yes."

What was this insensitive un-reconstructed male doing in my car!

I changed the radio station to another that specialized in music. The sound of Rod Stewart and 'Maggie May' came out of the speakers. This time Peter approved.

"Do you remember this song? It was popular when we were in London. I really liked it. I used to envy Rod Stewart his hair."

"And I suppose his blonde girlfriends?"

"Well, yes. But you were blonde then. I remember there was another song you and your girlfriends used to sing in the pub after a few beers. Some bird song?. And you used to go through actions as well."

"The chicken dance?"

"No, chirpy something."

Oh dear, that would have been 'Chirpy, Chirpy, Cheep, Cheep'. It was on the radio when I was first in England and we girls used to sing it and wave our hands around after a few beers, well probably after the fourth beer.

For lunch we found a fish and chip shop and bought seafood takeaways and some drinks, walked down towards the beach and sat on the grass and ate, surrounded by seagulls and the salt air.

"Why are you smiling?"

Peter's unexpected smile had surprised me. When he smiles his usual serious, even grumpy, look softens and he can look so gentle.

"I'm just thinking of your description of yourself as 'Little Miss Organised'. I remember when I met you I always thought you were so in control and so confident. It was something I found attractive about you. Nothing seemed to faze you. You always had an answer or knew what to do or where to go."

Little did Peter know what I was really like. Perhaps I had been like that once, but when he showed up I changed. I was in England, doing all the things I had read about and dreamt about. Yet suddenly I wasn't sure. Did I throw it all up and go back to Australia with him? I guess Miss Organised came to the fore and my head over-ruled my heart. That was why I ran away to Germany. I wasn't going to change my plans. Even my marriage had been a bit like that. Everybody said Tony was a great catch and he was. He was fun for a while, until he needed fresh conquests. Again I think my head had over-ruled my heart but you make the best of it.

"Why was Billy near Ballarat if he was going to Melbourne? Which way would you normally go to Melbourne from Oakleigh?"

I explained to Peter that usually we would go through Geelong. You could go up to Ballarat, but it is longer and out of the way, unless you are heading north somewhere. You can also go the way we were driving along the coast but again it is longer and slower."

"Why did everyone think he was going to Melbourne?"

"Well he had friends in Melbourne. He liked the pubs and nightlife around Carlton. Merry was in Melbourne, he often crashed at her flat. I don't think anyone gave it too much thought because Merry was missing. It just seemed the likely thing he would do."

"Did any of his friends know he was coming to Melbourne?"

"I don't think so, nobody mentioned anything but of course all the attention was on Merry's disappearance."

"Did anyone say they phoned him that night?"

"Not that I know."

"So perhaps he wasn't going to Melbourne after all. Do you think he might have been planning to meet Merry somewhere, say Ballarat?"

"I don't know. Why would she go to Ballarat? If it was her on the phone to Oakleigh why wouldn't he have said it was her? Besides she usually talked to her parents if she phoned. Anyway she would have been in Melbourne."

"We don't really know that. She had gone missing Friday after work. It's just nobody had missed her for a day or so. By then Billy was dead. She could have called him. Perhaps she had a problem that she didn't want the rest of the family to know about."

"You're being very melodramatic! I saw her not long before she disappeared and she was fine. Happy and bubbly as usual. No problems."

"Did she have any aggrieved boyfriends, jilted lovers, secret admirers?"

"No, she wasn't that sort of person. She had lots of friends but there was no big romance with any one. They were all just friends. Why are you so interested?"

"I suppose it's my nature, curiosity. I'm always attracted to problems. Perhaps that's why I became an engineer: to solve problems."

"Have you tried crosswords?"

He gave me a look. I half expected him to say he found them too easy. Would he like jigsaw puzzles and scrabble?

"Why did you become a mining engineer?"

"I wasn't smart enough to be a doctor. Besides I would

have hated the responsibility for people's lives. Law didn't appeal. Either arguing over petty details that have little real importance, or doing wills and property conveyancing. I couldn't be a teacher. I lacked the patience. My father worked in the office of a transport business and I guess I wanted something outside. Little did I realise that most of my mining would be underground or in an office as well."

"You never thought about the land."

"No. That was just so outside of my world to even consider. We didn't even have any family who lived in the country. I was a city boy and mining offered a way out. After I started my course I found I enjoyed the problem solving involved in the actual mining. It interested me more than, say, geology. What about you? Why did you become a teacher?"

"It seemed to be what lots of girls did in those days. You became a teacher, or a nurse, or took a job in an office or shop. I enjoyed my time at school. I liked learning new things and having the companionship of my school friends. There weren't many girls my age in the bush. I was also fortunate to have a teacher who was a great role model and encouraged me to go to Teacher's College. It was only when I was in England that I found another, more interesting career. I guess after handling a class of unruly boys business men were easy!"

Peter went quiet as we finished our fish and chips.

"Let's go back to Ballarat."

"Why?"

"There is just something—I don't know what. Just something, a part of the puzzle but I don't even know what part.   Perhaps it is something we have seen!   Merry disappeared on Friday afternoon. Billy gets a phone call on Saturday night. He is upset and leaves in a rush. Later that night he is killed in a car accident near Ballarat. It is not the usual road he would take to go to Melbourne. Then you have a bad feeling about a hotel in the city."

"I didn't think you would place much emphasis on woman's intuition! By the time we get there it will be too late to do anything."

"Have you got any plans for tomorrow?"

I hadn't, but I wasn't sure whether this was genuine curiosity, or something else. Did I really want to spend more time with this man?

"Well?"

"What are your plans?"

"We go back to Ballarat. We retrace our steps and see what happens. I'll take you out to a good dinner this evening."

This was looking like something else.

"Two rooms!"

"Of course. I'm not trying to lead you astray."

I wasn't sure I liked the answer. At least he could have made a play.

6 BALLARAT AGAIN

Suzie

I had never driven from Lorne to Ballarat. Looking at the map it seemed the easiest and quickest way would be to continue towards Geelong and then take the highway to Ballarat. Otherwise it would mean taking a secondary road across the Otway Range and a drive north on minor roads. The highway seemed the best and quickest option.

As we drove towards Ballarat I felt a sense of unease creeping over me. I didn't know if it was because of Peter, or if there was something else. He appeared to have no idea what we were looking for when we arrived in the city. The image of a bloodhound rushing around searching for a scent came to my mind. Yet the unease continued to grow the closer we came to the city.

By the time we arrived in Ballarat it was late afternoon. As we drove into the city Peter looked for motels. Every motel had a 'no vacancy' sign displayed. A banner across the road gave the reason. It was the Begonia Festival. We had decided to come to the city on one of the busiest weekends of the year. Finally Peter spotted an old tired looking motel that still showed 'vacancy'. We stopped, and he went in to the reception desk.

He came back to the car.

"The receptionist says they have one room available. It has twin beds. Every other room in Ballarat has been booked by garden clubs for months. I think we should take it. I can sleep in the car."

The thought of me asking Peter to spend the night sleeping in the car seemed rather cruel. His offer was generous but nights in Ballarat could get cold at this time of the year, and while we may have all slept in cars when we were younger, these days I prefer a comfortable bed. I was sure Peter would feel the same way.

"I guess if it is the only room we can manage."

I remembered times in Europe when a whole group of us would bunk in together. We mostly managed to look the other way to allow for people's privacy. We even arranged to be away for a period of time to give some people a chance for more intimate moments. Just thinking about it I realised friends had done that for me several times. When I was with Peter. I wonder whether he remembers.

"We had better take it but I can't have you out in the car. I would feel so guilty being warm and knowing how cold and uncomfortable you would be."

"I hoped you would say that. I wasn't looking forward to it. I promise I will be well behaved."

Peter

It is a long time since I had shared a room with a woman other than my wife, and that is quite different. You are

55

already familiar with each other and know their ways. Which one snores, which one gets up for a cup of tea at two o'clock. Back in London it was so different. We wanted to be with each other and to feel our bodies wrapped together. Then there was no thought about modesty. I wonder what her body is like now. Will she still wear those short nighties I remember she used to wear? It will be strange lying in a separate bed in the same room after all these years. I wonder if she remembers, so much has happened since then.

"Our hostess has recommended a small restaurant up near Sovereign Hill. She thinks it would be best to phone and check, in case they are full. Then we could change and go and find it."

Suzie

The receptionist's suggestion was wise. The restaurant near Sovereign Hill appeared to be popular with locals. Without Peter's phone reservation we would not have been able to have a table. It was only a small restaurant but the food was beautiful and the staff informal and friendly. We sat and ate and drank and talked. The conversation ranged over many subjects. Peter was great company and I found even when I disagreed strongly with him we still accepted each other's view. He was however quite conservative in his opinions. I realised talking with him that I was actually much more conservative than I sometimes admitted, especially to my daughter.

When the time came to return to our room I couldn't help but wonder what pyjamas he would wear. Would they be silky boxers or would he have full length flannelette jamis? Perhaps he didn't wear pyjamas. That would complicate our sleeping arrangements. What would he think of mine? I had packed a full length warm nighty for the visit to Oakleigh but hadn't expected to be wearing it in front of a man. Perhaps it would look a bit frumpy. If I had known I would have packed a special pair of silk pyjamas—they could cover most eventualities and most of the body!

I needn't have worried. I changed and was in my bed while Peter stood outside looking around the street. He seemed deep in thought. Eventually he came in, changed in the bathroom and went to his bed. I had difficulty keeping a straight face. He was wearing full length cotton pyjamas patterned with multi-coloured elephants. I wondered whether he had bought them himself, or if his wife had bought them for him. Perhaps they were a present from his son.

Peter

I lay in bed listening to Suzie's breathing. She was already asleep. Standing outside I had thought about what we were doing. I'd met a girlfriend I knew from so many years ago in my past, and invited her to join me on a visit to a city I had always wanted to see. Next I am off to the Western district to visit one of her oldest friends and now we are sharing a bedroom, separate beds this time, and on some quest to find a girl that went missing forty-one years ago. It was ridiculous! All we had to work with was some bad feeling she had about a hotel and the strange idea that I had seen the answer and it was in this city. Nothing more. Nothing really to work with. Was I just doing it because I wanted to spend time with her? I certainly did enjoy her company, but she had been unreliable in the past and had disappeared on me once before. What was next? I guess check out the hotel again, and see where that leads. Perhaps walking the street will give us a clue. It is all so unlikely. Perhaps we should just view the begonias.

Next morning Suzie drove to the railway station and we left the car in the parking lot. We started to retrace our steps. We crossed the railway line and turned into Lydiard Street. At Sturt Street we turned again intending to visit the Grande Imperial. As we passed a bookshop I stopped. I now realised what had caught my attention on our first visit. Suzie had gone into the bookshop to buy a magazine for the train trip home and I had stayed outside idly reading a display of old newspaper headlines pasted over the window. Somebody had decided that it would be an effective way of screening off the back of a display case. It was one headline that had intrigued me: 'Disappearance Mystery, Girl returns'. The date on the paper was May 1968.

Rather than go to the Grande we decided to visit the city library. Fortunately they were open on a Saturday morning and as I hoped they had a collection of old newspapers on microfiche. We tracked down the newspaper headline in the window. It told the story of a young girl who had been reported missing when staying with the family of a school friend. Three days later she was back with her own family. Police had investigated but her family had not wished to proceed with further enquiries. The only information from the girl was that two men had blindfolded her and taken her somewhere and locked her in a room. The room was very cold and there were no windows. Apparently she had been well cared for, the men had given her blankets and food and she was not otherwise distressed. There were no more details and the police had ceased their investigation.

"Do you think that may have anything to do with Merry?"

Suzie thought about my question.

"If it had been my daughter I would have wanted the kidnapper found and off the street. It was years before Merry disappeared. This girl was fourteen, Merry was twenty-one. The girl reappeared, Merry didn't. This girl was local. Merry was from Melbourne. It seems unlikely unless there is some other connection. I don't think your hunch is much help."

"It is strange that the family didn't want the police to investigate. I'm sure you would if it was your daughter."

"Yes, I definitely would want some answers. Perhaps they knew more than they admitted to the police. Perhaps there was some dispute within the family or with some business associates."

"Do you think there might have been something like that with the Olivers? Perhaps blackmail?"

Suzie had known the Olivers from when she was a young girl. While they certainly didn't discuss family affairs or business dealings publicly they didn't seem to be the sort of family with terrible secrets, and she couldn't imagine them being blackmailed. Merry was always so open and they had shared their lives like sisters. There was nothing there that would indicate blackmail. Her only secrets were probably with her brother. Still sometimes the most outgoing people hide secrets and the most reserved people have nothing to hide.

"It is possible, but I think it is very unlikely. I don't think there is anything to work with in that story. Let's see if we can find out something about Billy's accident."

It was not hard to follow up on Suzie's suggestion. Billy had been killed on Saturday and the following Monday there was a report in the paper. His car had been heading towards Ballarat, and west of Scarsdale had run off the road and hit a tree. His crashed car was seen by a passing motorist. The driver had left his passenger with Billy and driven back to Scarsdale to get help. By the time an ambulance arrived it was too late. The report stated that it appeared the car had been travelling very fast. Conditions that night were bad. It was very wet and windy and that section of road had a reputation for accidents due to the bad bends. It seemed Billy had been driving too fast, on a bad section of road, on a black wet night. There was no suggestion of any other cause for an accident.

"What about checking out the history of the hotel? Perhaps there might be some stories that give us a lead."

Suzie's suggestion was easier to make than do. Where to start! The hotel had been there for over one hundred years. What would get it mentioned in the newspapers? What were we even looking for? While I was pondering these questions Suzie used her female logic and asked the librarian. The first librarian was obliging but had no suggestions apart from passing us onto a colleague. Her colleague was much more helpful. She had an interest in local history. We were looking in the wrong newspaper. Ballarat had had many newspapers over its lifetime. Most had come and gone while the Courier continued on. Back in the late sixties there had been an upstart paper that had commenced and taken up community issues. One of the issues was a gambling den in Ballarat. It had quickly become the talk of the district. Each week the newspaper had made increasingly direct but still veiled allegations of corruption and police payoffs. Standover men had threatened the editor. While it never mentioned who was involved or where the gambling was being conducted, all the locals had their own theories and a number of venues were nominated. Half the town wanted the paper closed down, the other half were unconcerned or supportive of the campaign to stop the gambling.

Then came news that police, 'acting on a citizen's complaint', had raided the Grande Imperial hotel. Apparently they broke down the door of an upstairs room and found twenty men from Melbourne holding a birthday party for one of their group. No indication of any gambling was found and the police were forced to apologise to the men and the hotel licensee. The next issue of the Examiner carried the story and an editorial. The editor described the whole thing as a fraud set up to hide the truth and make the police look as if they were taking action. This brought a defamation action from the licensee of the Grande. The case was settled out of court but eventually the newspaper closed and the editor left town. Even more helpful our librarian tracked down the editorial dated 1970. There was also a grainy indistinct photo of the licensee of the hotel standing in front of the hotel door. The same door we had walked though on our visit to the Grande Imperial.

On Suzie's suggestion we decided to drive out and have a look at the scene of Billy's accident. Mrs Oliver had not been very definite about the location, mentioning only a very winding section of road with trees close to its edge. The newspaper article had been more helpful fixing the site two and a half to three kilometres west of Scarsdale. That still left a number of possible corners that could have been the crash site but the newspaper photo of the crashed car narrowed the site down to the fatal bend. Over the years some of the trees in the photo had grown and a few closer to the road had been removed. It would appear Billy must have lost control of the car on a bend, run down an embankment and hit a tree.

"May I have a look at the map?"

Suzie handed me the map.

"If Billy was on this road he would not be going to Melbourne unless he was going somewhere else first. It is the long way from Oakleigh. From here he would have to go to Ballarat then down the Western Highway to Melbourne, or he could turn off just before Ballarat and go to Geelong and then to Melbourne and that's even further. I don't think he was going to Melbourne."

"Do you think he was going to Ballarat?"

"Possibly. Or further on. Given we know the time when he left the Olivers, and the time of the accident here, he must have been driving very fast all the way from Oakleigh. He wouldn't have had time to stop anywhere and still be here at the time he crashed. Besides if he was driving that fast it suggests he hadn't got to where he wanted to be. I've seen enough. When you're ready let's go and check out the Grande again."

Unlike our last visit the lounge of Grande Imperial was noisy and full of people. Even the aroma of the hotel had changed with floral scents overpowering the smell of stale beer. Every chair and table was occupied, mostly by women with only a few men present. None were young. I thought Suzie and I were probably the youngest people in the room apart from the same few regular drinkers who had arrived for their daily session as they had done during our previous visit. They were huddled, seemingly in fear, down one end of the bar. Obviously the Lismore garden club, whose bus was parked outside, had taken over the hotel for their trip to view the begonias.

Suzie and I found stools and sat at the opposite end of the bar to the regulars. The same surly barman who had served us earlier in the week served us again, pretending not to recognise us. We ordered our drinks and watched the other guests. I wondered what the ladies of the garden club would make of the hotel and our surly host. He certainly didn't appear to want to make people welcome on what should have been his most profitable week of the year. I could imagine the reports to the next club meeting. I wondered if begonia fanciers were as puritanical as some of the women in Claire's 'The Antipodean Society for Australian Native Plants'. Some of them had an almost religious fervour and viewed exotic plants as the church viewed heretics during the Inquisition. Then I remembered why we were here.

"How do you feel about the hotel this time? Do you still have the bad feeling you had on our last visit?"

"This is my third time here and each time has been different. It was such a different crowd on Merry's and my visit. Not all old people like now. This time it is noisy and happy but the first time, while it was busy, it was quiet. People seemed preoccupied. I don't know if they were worried about what may happen or what had happened. It wasn't relaxed like this afternoon. Tonight with the room full of people it has such a different feel. Even the horrid mix of furniture doesn't look as bad when the chairs have people sitting on them."

The barman returned to refill our glasses and I thought it would be an opportunity to find out more about the hotel. As

I suspected he was also the licensee. He had been in the hotel for ten years but when I asked him about the owner he just said he didn't know anything. Some company owned it. He just dealt with an agent in Melbourne. He paid the rent and looked after the place. From the faded look of the hotel neither he nor the owners were greatly interested in maintenance.

When I brought up the story of the gambling raid that Suzie and I had discovered in our library research he denied any knowledge of gambling at the hotel. After I pointed out the story related to forty-two years ago his defensive attitude eased. I had the feeling he thought we were referring to more recent times. Perhaps he did have Friday night card games in an upstairs room. When I asked when the hotel had last changed hands he again brought up the Melbourne agent. He didn't know who the company was. Could have even been overseas owners. Sometimes overseas investors bought property. It was strange, I was sure there would have to be a lease agreement and the owners name would be on that. There would probably even be an owner's address, although that might just be a lawyer's or accountant's office. Simple curiosity should have been enough to ask the managing agent for some background to the owner. It seemed unusual for a licensee not to have some idea about the owner of his hotel. I got the definite feeling that my questions were not welcome.

After he left I suggested to Suzie that she might be able to use her feminine wiles to extract some more information.

"Thank you! Am I supposed to be Mata Hari? Do I go to bed with him?"

"No. No need to go that far. Just bat your eyelids, smile,

do whatever women do. I'll go and have a chat to those ladies and see what we should do tomorrow. Buy me another beer please."

I left and went over to four ladies standing together. They were busily discussing the merits of growing roses. One even had her mobile phone out showing a picture of a special bloom. They were welcoming and for five minutes informed me of what we should see and not see at the Festival. From the corner of my eye I could see Suzie chatting with the barman. When he left I returned to her.

"How did it go?"

"I guess my charm is not as great as you think. I asked about the history of the hotel and he was no use. Then I asked about any crimes or bad happenings that may have taken place in the hotel and he told me I ask too many questions, he was very busy and walked off."

"Well I guess that's all we will find out here. Where will we go for dinner tonight?"

"Peter, this time it's my shout. I think, knowing you, we had better make it a steak house."

There was still so much I didn't know about this woman. What did she like now? Did she have expensive tastes? She obviously wasn't worried about money and she dressed well. Was she wealthy? I didn't even know what she did or where she lived.

Suzie

I was glad Peter had decided to take a taxi from our motel to our dinner. It was so much more relaxing not to have to count the drinks as you would if you were going to drive. Not that I am a big drinker, but the last thing I want is to be stopped and given an alcohol test, and lose my licence. The restaurant was dark, crowded and old-fashioned, but our steaks were beautifully cooked and flavoursome and it was obvious why the restaurant was so popular with locals. Unlike our meal the night before, where we had covered a broad range of subjects, tonight's conversation was much more personal.

Peter talked of his years working in mines. He had been at university during the days of the Vietnam War and had been in the birthday ballot for National Service in the army. His birthday had not come up in the ballot so he had finished his studies and then found his first permanent mining job. He had sometimes wondered how life might have been different if he had been called up to do his National Service training. While he could have deferred the training until he finished his degree, he would then have had to do his two years in the army. It was unlikely he would have travelled to the UK, we would never have met, and probably he would not have been in Africa at the same time as his future wife. Perhaps he would never have met Claire. One decision, or event, and our lives can take a very different path.

I asked him if he was politically active when he was at university. The war and conscription were such charged issues at that time. Unlike many students, especially the university ones I knew, he was not protesting in the streets. He was relieved when he was not called up and really would not have wanted to fight in Vietnam, but if it had happened, then so be it. He had always been suspicious of the communists in Russia and China and could not understand how some university students had been so believing of the supposed policies of the communists. To him Stalin and

Mao had brought great suffering to their people.

He seemed to want to bring me into talking of my life in England and since my return to Australia. If I am asked personal questions I usually skirt the answers, and I did with Peter. I guess by my nature I am basically a private person. However as the night went on Peter's openness affected me and I found myself answering more of his questions. We ended the night with a very good brandy and called a taxi to take us back to our motel room with the two beds.

We slept in on Sunday morning. The sun was up when we woke and it was a beautiful day. Peter suggested it might be best if we went for a walk, found somewhere for breakfast, and then looked at the Festival displays. I suggested we drive, so we checked out of our motel and drove to the Lake. There was no parking available. By the time I found somewhere to leave the car we could have walked from the motel. I didn't tell Peter his idea had been the better one. Over a coffee we discussed our investigations. We had discovered nothing. Billy's accident was from driving too fast. No links to Merry. A hotel with a questionable past, and an unfriendly present. Nothing to link it to Merry. As far as detectives went we were definitely amateurs, and not very successful ones at that.

Ballarat was famous for its begonias. Plant collections were the great status symbol of its heyday. Just as rich aristocrats and industrialists in Britain filled their estates with exotic flowers, Ballarat used its new found gold riches to create a Botanic Garden to reflect its wealth. Within seven years of the first discovery of gold the Botanic Garden was laid out and then the avenue of Giant Redwoods planted. Over the years more wonderful and rare plants were introduced. A conservatory was built and stocked full of the latest exotic specimens from South America. That interest in begonias was on show in the maze of flowers hanging from the walls and sitting on benches and the floor in the latest conservatory. Together we walked and admired the variety of blooms and plants on display with their beautiful coloured flowers and leaves. While Peter walked the Prime Minister's Avenue with its sculptures of Australian political leaders, I shopped at the plant stalls and found myself needing help to carry my new purchases back to the car. Last night Peter had questioned me on my interests. Today I think he had an answer.

The trip back to Melbourne was quiet. Neither of us talked much, we both knew that he would be returning to Sydney the next day. I dropped him off at his friend's house, and as I was about to drive away I realised I didn't have his phone number, nor had I given him mine. We exchanged numbers, a brief hug and separated. The afternoon seemed to get colder.

7 MELBOURNE ENQUIRIES

Suzie

Thursday was bridge club afternoon. I decided to go. I was often asked by friends if I enjoyed playing bridge and I always answered equivocally. I wasn't as dedicated as some of the players who took their bridge games very seriously and were sometimes terse to the point of rudeness with newcomers who made errors. However I did like the stimulation it gave my mind and had made friends with a few of the players. What I especially enjoyed was the after-play early dinners that some of the less serious members had at nearby Thai or Italian restaurants. It was a fun group with lots of chat and gossip and some interesting discussion. I enjoyed that more than the cards.

I really needed something to take my mind off Peter. Our parting had been formal, and I kept thinking of the last time I had seen him in the UK. Then, I had been the one to run away. This time I wasn't sure what I wanted, or if I wanted to see him again. Our farewell had been very open-ended. Perhaps it would be the last time I would see him, perhaps not. But then did I want to see him again? It was a strange feeling. One that I hadn't had for longer than I cared to remember. I did have to admit to myself that I had enjoyed my time with Peter.

Besides, I hadn't been very honest about my marriage. It had ended as I had said, but I had glossed over the problems and hurt I had felt. There was a lot that I had left unsaid. Some years after Peter I had been attracted to Tony, and this time the life fitted my dreams. Tony had romanced me and I had fallen for him. He was certainly attractive, in both personality and looks. As I found out a few years into the marriage there were many other women who also fell for his charms, and he had obliged many of them.

Once our babies arrived he had become more inclined to wander and the various conferences he attended provided opportunities. When it became more blatant we moved to separate bedrooms.

Tony was always a good provider. While he indulged his lady friends it never took away from his support for his children, or for me. I guess the children and I provided him with the appearance of respectability that was good for business, plus a handy shield if the demands of the latest girlfriend became too insistent. I had heard he claimed he couldn't leave me because of the kids. I used to worry as to whether I hung in for the kids or because I enjoyed the lifestyle. There were family holidays skiing in Switzerland, holidays in the south of France or Spain and one year to Essaouira on the coast of Morocco. I had the freedom to lunch with my friends and we had weekends away as a family. Our arrangement was common knowledge. My girlfriends supported me. A few were in the same situation. Once the children were in school I had gone back to my old job on a part-time basis. I did feel uncomfortable with my life but I kept saying, 'it was for the kids'. I wasn't sure I was being honest with myself—the fringe benefits were certainly appealing.

Word had gotten around and the unpleasant part was fending off some of his friends and associates who assumed I was fair game and would be available. It may have been London in the late seventies and early eighties, and while the swinging sixties had left their mark, at heart I was still a county girl from the Riverina.

In some ways I felt I was a kept woman, although I had no demands made on me. Tony liked the mantle of respectability a wife gave him. It suited his position and it was only when Judith arrived that it changed. At first it was a meeting that ran into the late evening, then it became several busy days with late nights and it would be more convenient for him to stay in town than travel home daily. That way he wouldn't disturb me with his very late return to our home and his early departure next morning. Eventually he had moved permanently into her flat in London and we saw much less of him. By this stage the children were at grammar school and well aware of our situation. My part-time work became full-time, and I loved the independence it gave me. Until then I had never admitted to my parents what my situation was. I thought they would never approve of my separation. I was sure their belief was that you married for life and worked at making it work.

When I finally told them I was surprised at their reaction. They had known for years that there was a problem but didn't want to broach the subject unless I did. When we finally separated and Tony moved in with Judith, my parents were very happy that at last I had my freedom.

I hadn't been much of a partner at the bridge table this afternoon—as one of the players very sharply informed me. My thoughts had kept returning to Peter and our time together in Ballarat and at Oakleigh, and I wasn't concentrating on the game in hand. Later at dinner at the restaurant I was sitting with Ian and Elizabeth Holmes. I had been to school with Elizabeth and we had stayed friends ever since. When I had returned to live permanently in Australia, Elizabeth had been a great support for me as I re-established my life in Melbourne. Her abrupt manner often frightened some people, but behind her directness she was a warm and caring personality. She had also been a friend of Merry and knew of her disappearance.

When I mentioned my trip to Ballarat and told them of my feelings at the hotel Ian's curiosity was piqued. Elizabeth was more interested in Peter. At different times some of my friends had tried to introduce me to single men. I had enjoyed the dinners but they had never gone further, and my friends had given up on any further introductions. At our age many of us had moved through divorces and the men had either gone for younger wives or had been quickly snapped up by the divorcees or widows out for a new husband. I had watched the aggressive hunting with both amusement and horror and had no wish to be involved.

Ian had lived all his life in Melbourne. He was well connected in business circles through the various enterprises he had run over the years. He always heard the gossip and rumours—sometimes true, sometimes false—which circulated in the business world. Over the years he had heard stories of illegal gambling, it moved around from place to place, and he had once heard of some place in Ballarat. He had never been interested and didn't know any details but he knew a chap who was very knowledgeable about such things. To call him a friend was perhaps too strong a connection, but then acquaintance was too weak. Roley was always great company but I got the feeling that Ian found extended periods with him exhausting.

Roley was of an old established family who preferred him to live somewhere else. That suited Roley, and he had moved around from Bali to Hong Kong and was now settled in Bangkok. His family preferred him to be out of sight. Apparently he returned occasionally to Melbourne, rumoured to collect another cheque to support his lifestyle and the numerous young ladies he knew. I had heard of the younger Roley and his reputation when I was at teachers college and had seen him at various parties, but I had never really known him. He was way out of my league and I, anyway, wasn't the type he liked. I did remember being introduced to him once at Naughton's pub in Parkville, and again later at one of the cheap Italian restaurants near the university where we students hung out, but his interest was more in the classier suburbs, or the ski fields of Buller, or down on the Peninsula. Either that, or girls with large bosoms.

Somehow, to the University's surprise, he had finished his Law Degree. Given his penchant for parties, horse racing, fast cars and skiing, it was unexpected. His legal skills had mostly been put to use getting himself or his friends out of trouble. He had quite a reputation around Melbourne and he had personally made several bookmakers rich with his gambling. If there was any gambling in Victoria, Roley would have known of it. He would be able to tell me more about the Grande Imperial but he was last known to be in Bangkok.

Several days later the phone rang. It was Ian. Roley was

in Melbourne. He had run into him at the golf club. Would I like to meet with him?

"Yes."

"I'll arrange it."

8 ROLEY

Suzie

An hour later the phone rang. Ian had been good to his word.

"Hello, it's Roley. Ian Holmes suggested I call you. What about dinner?" I sensed that any dinner with Roley could be a problem so instead suggested lunch, to which he agreed. We arranged to meet in a small restaurant in Lygon Street.

He wasn't what I remembered or expected. He was carrying a little more weight than the last time I saw him. That was forty plus years ago! Now his hair was trimmed shorter, the mop of blonde hair touching the collar had gone and grey showed around the ears and temple. Gone also were the tight polyester pants with flares and the shirts with big collars. In his sports coat and slacks he could have been an old-fashioned grazier from my past. He looked far from the colourful gambling identity and lady's man of repute. He did still have the easy, open smile and bright outgoing disposition that had made him so popular at parties all those years ago. Without any conscious effort on my part I felt myself warm to him. He was certainly charming. I could see something of my husband, ex-husband, in him, but while Tony always liked a veneer of respectability in his lady friends and expected them to be 'classy', Roley was more interested in attractive young women, good sex and fun company.

He selected a bottle of Vasse Felix chardonnay from Western Australia and invited me to order.

The conversation was light and enjoyable. His stories were amusing, and he had a way of involving you. Suddenly you realised you were talking with him as if you had known him for years.

He had an innocence that was at odds with the life he lived. In a way he was something of an aging hippy—without cares or ties, seeking some perfect place that was not yet found by the tourists. I could see him in a sarong, holding a bintang, overlooking the rice paddies of Ubud in Bali, but I could also see him on a boat on the harbour of Hong Kong with a G & T in his hand. Somehow the ageing man across the table from me still had a little of that carefree spirit. But not for him the earth-mothers of Nimbin. Roley also wanted the comforts and luxuries of the world. The boat on Hong Kong harbour would have to be a fancy cruiser.

He no longer lived in Bangkok. The traffic had become so bad it was impossible. Besides the flooding from the klongs was becoming worse. He loved the people so he had found a beautiful hideaway. It was away from the beach area and reminded him of parts of Bali of so many years ago, before the tourist hordes arrived.

I was intrigued by his life. He told me he still did some work for various businessmen. He knew lots of people, who knew lots of people, and sometimes he arranged meetings for them. He still had an office in Hong Kong. Some of his clients used it when they needed a local address or residency for business reasons. 'A bit like a post box really' as he explained it. Actually he had a very smart girl who looked after all the business there. He only had to visit occasionally. She was very capable and good looking. I thought any woman who worked for Roley would have to be good looking. He really was a sleaze but he was good company.

He told stories of watching the Thais using elephants in the forest to drag out timber for milling. He had been fortunate to be in Thailand and attend a ceremony when the King had been presented with a new 'White Elephant'. These elephants were sacred and a symbol of royal power in Thailand. There were not really white, but had paler skin than usual. They could be albino, although not necessarily so. Some were even called 'Pink Elephants'! Apparently there were various grades and the King could refuse the lower grades. Roley told a story of how a King would give a 'White Elephant' to someone who displeased him. Since it was sacred it could not be put to work, but it still had to be maintained and cared for and so was a great financial burden to the owner. This could even cause the recipient to suffer bankruptcy. It was sometimes used as a way for early Thai Kings to harm their enemies. The present King has ten 'White Elephants' which the Thai people considered a great achievement.

His elephant stories led on to other adventures he had had in his travels. One story was of sailing in the Aegean Sea when he and some friends had swum across from their sailing boat and breakfasted at a little village in Turkey without legally entering the country. It brought back memories of my backpacking days in Greece and the times spent camped on beaches or staying in little inns in tiny island villages so many years ago. I suddenly felt envious of the young tanned backpackers making their way around Australia. So many memories of times past!

Roley was entertaining company and we were having dessert before I realised I hadn't raised the subject of my trip to Ballarat. Had he ever heard of the Grande Imperial?

Yes, he knew of the Grande Imperial. He had stayed there a few times many years ago.

I mentioned that there were rumours that it had been a secret gambling den.

"Yes, that was true," he said. It was far enough away from Melbourne not to raise concern with the police and wowsers but close enough to get there easily. He had visited a few times to play blackjack. They were very obliging and didn't ask too many questions. I assumed that meant they didn't notice the different Mrs Roleys who accompanied him to the hotel.

According to Roley the gambling was accessed from the hotel. He remembered you went through a sort of tunnel and came to the large room with the various tables and card games. It was all very well set up and very smart. He knew some of the clientele; he had acted for some of them in various matters. Having heard of Roley's legal practice from Ian Holmes I wondered just what the matters may have involved. Roley had never been seen in a court and nobody had ever used him for conveyancing. Ian had hinted that a few of the clients that Roley assisted were sometimes thought to be less than reputable, although there had never been any allegations of misconduct in his legal affairs.

There was a very good bar and there always seemed to be

attractive young ladies around. There was something about the lift. There was a man who operated it. There was something else different about it. It looked as if it was going up but when you stepped out you were in a room with no windows and it felt as if you were going down.

He had only gone a few times. He had doubts about how honest the games were. Horse races and jockeys were not always honest but at least you had a chance. He reckoned those table games gave the house an unfair advantage.

Did he know Merry and Billy Oliver?

He remembered meeting Billy at various parties, but Billy was younger and he didn't really know him. He was at the Grande both times he had visited. Billy seemed to be well known and looked like he was losing both times.

"I thought he must have had a good supply of cash. I lost a lot but I reckon he would have lost more."

The man who ran it went on to bigger things in business. There was a story about some fuss or something. Some local wowser group was causing political trouble and the police had raided the hotel but found nothing. Then he had heard the gambling had been shut down suddenly a few years later and the hotel was sold. Perhaps there was more trouble with the police, or perhaps the wrong person was getting the payoff.

"What was the boss like?"

"Very obliging, until you crossed him. It was said he could turn nasty if you didn't pay your debts, which he very obligingly let you run up."

Roley had never got in that situation but it was rumoured

that if you didn't pay up then your wife or girlfriend, even your kids, could disappear for a few days until you paid. He remembered seeing a huge, giant of a man in the gaming room both times he visited. Nobody knew exactly what it was he did, but it was rumoured that he was the enforcer or the boss's minder. He didn't know his name but gamblers called him 'The Bear', or 'The Bull', or something like that.

I told him the story of the young girl who had disappeared and reappeared, and asked him if it could have had something to do with the gambling.

"I've no idea. I never heard of any actual cases. It was always just rumour. Probably the owner liked to have a dangerous reputation. It made people more likely to pay up on their losses."

"Who was he?"

"Nobody ever mentioned his name. People were afraid of him and he kept a low profile. Unlike a lot of gamblers he didn't gamble himself. It was just business for him. I did see him later in Melbourne. It was after the casino had closed and he had gone respectable. He was doing very well. It was a good time to be in real estate development with the city growing. He is now a very important businessman in this city and in other states and overseas as well. If you cross him you can run into difficulties doing business. I also gather he has some friends you do not want to know but that happens in some industries."

"What's his name?"

"You don't need to know. It is better not to know. If you do ever come across him it would be better not to know about his past. If I told you his name, you would think about his past every time you see his photo in a newspaper, or magazine, or on the television. I'm sure he does not like his early years mentioned. It doesn't look good with his charity donations and respectability and new friends. I suspect he is the sort of person you would not want to have anything to do with anyway. I don't think it is a good idea to ask too many questions about him. Now my lady, what about this afternoon then dinner tonight and a nightcap?"

The Roley of repute had appeared. Reputedly never one to let any opportunity go by! I remembered once being told that if you asked often enough your chance of success was higher. I thought that with me Roley was probably operating from habit. I was sure I wasn't his usual type of well-endowed young lady of a certain character. Since it was still only three in the afternoon I wondered what the rest of the afternoon might involve. Still I had enjoyed his company, Roley might be a sleaze but he was good fun. There could be some pleasure in an afternoon of love with him. Well not love exactly, more like lust, although I could hardly see Roley and me tearing the clothes off each other, more like—just sex. With his experience and mistresses I was sure I could pick up something from Roley. Well, perhaps that's not quite the way I should phrase it!

I politely used the excuse of having to baby-sit my grandchild.

As I left Roley gave me his business card.

"Give me a call if you come to Thailand. My Thai address is on one side, the other side is the Hong Kong office. There are some lovely restaurants near where I live that I would love to show you. You would enjoy them."

That night I wondered whether I should phone Peter with

my information. I decided it would be better not to call him. I spent the night regretting my decision.

9 OX

Suzie

When I woke next morning Roley's 'giant' was on my mind.

I had been restless all night. In my mind disturbing images of Ballarat goldfields, a giant of a man, Peter, and a dark building were swirling in and out of my consciousness. A shadowy image of a police car kept appearing, and disappearing before reappearing again. Two vague women were also mixed into the dream, or nightmare. I felt that somehow they must be me and Merry. I had no idea what the re-occurring images meant, but they were unsettling, and I felt they presaged bad times for Peter and me.

The dream brought back memories. I recalled that I had seen such a man when I was staying at the Grande Imperial with Merry. Each day I had seen him. A huge man sitting alone, sitting quietly in a chair in the Lounge as if he was waiting for someone or something. He was wearing a suit but somehow didn't seem to be comfortable wearing it. In the evening he was absent. Perhaps he had gone to work in the gambling room that Roley had described.

I decided to visit Ballarat again to see if I could find him. Perhaps he could offer a clue to Merry's disappearance. I had no idea how he would be connected with Merry but for some unknown reason I felt I had to follow my feeling. It all seemed rather pointless. I couldn't see any connection but the feeling was persistent.

The day was cold, wet, and miserable as I drove alone to Ballarat—so unlike my visits with Peter. I wondered how I would find the man. I was sure Roley knew the name of the Boss but he certainly wasn't going to tell it to me. Besides I doubted that the Boss would be forthcoming with any information.

With a body like his, 'The Giant' could have been in a football team, or maybe he was a boxer. Perhaps there would be old photos on the wall of the 'Sportman's Bar' at the hotel. He must be old now. He hadn't been young, perhaps around forty or forty-five when I had seen him. I recalled a touch of grey around his temples. That would make him eighty or eighty-five now. He is probably dead. Still, perhaps I could find some clue as to what had happened to Merry. For some reason I associated her disappearance with Ballarat although again there was no obvious link to justify my feeling.

It was ten o'clock when I parked the car near the hotel and walked across to the Grande Imperial's entrance. Standing there in front of the once elegant but now somewhat tired looking doorway, I was again overcome with a sense of dread. The same feeling of dread I had felt on a previous visit, only this time it was more intense. In the grey wet morning the hotel stood dark and brooding over the street. Even the lovely cast iron lace work on the balcony didn't lighten the look but seemed more like teeth ready to consume. Then the sun came out and the mood lightened but the sense of dread remained. I stood there. I just could not bring myself to enter.

"What now?"

I was still wrapped in the feeling of dread as I found a café, ordered a coffee and pondered the question I had asked myself. I had come this far, there must be some other way to find this huge man. Then the library came to mind. It had worked for Peter and me on our second visit. The old newspapers would be sure to have stories about local football games, or perhaps some boxing bouts. From his age it would be the late nineteen forties or early fifties when he would have been at his peak.

I decided that my best, or quickest chance, would be to concentrate on the Sunday or Monday sports sections of the newspapers. It would be the likely place to find photos and reports of the weekend matches. I would probably only need to look from April to September for the football season. I hoped he was a local, otherwise the search would prove fruitless.

After hours of searching I finally came across a photo and an associated news article. There was the man, standing head and shoulders over his team mates and opposition players. He played for Creswick and in the article was called 'Ox'. His proper name was Frank O'Hartigan. I checked the telephone directory. There were no O'Hartigans in Ballarat or Creswick.

On an impulse I decided to take a drive to Creswick. It was only a short drive although in the days that Ox played football the city of Ballarat would not have stretched out so far along the Creswick road. Even the industrial and commercial buildings beyond the old cemetery would not have existed when Merry and I had visited Ballarat.

The road to Creswick led through farming and forestry country to the small town with its tree lined streets. I had decided my best chance of finding more information would be either the post office or the newsagent. Perhaps there might even be a historical society who could help.

The newsagent was pay dirt. "Go and see Dot, she may be able to help. She is in the nursing home."

The nurse took me to Dorothy O'Hartigan. Once she would have been a strapping young girl but now she was a frail old lady sitting in an armchair, a plaid rug across her knees, in a sunny corner of the nursing home sitting-room.

I had decided my approach would be to say I was writing a story on sporting teams of the past and the name Frank O'Hartigan, Ox, had come up. I wanted to learn more about him. I hoped such an approach would be more likely to encourage her conversation.

"Frank was my brother. He was three years younger than me, he was my little brother. At least until he started to grow, but even when he stopped he was still my little brother. He got the name Ox at school 'cause he was so strong. They always wanted him in the football teams but he wasn't very good at schoolwork—a bit like me."

"Did you have many brothers and sisters?"

"There were eight of us all up. Frank was the youngest, then me. The others all moved on. I'm the only one left now."

"Have you always lived in Creswick?"

"Yes. I looked after Mum and Dad until they died. I never married so it was my job. My two sisters married and left town. I stayed. Maybe that was why I didn't marry. I had a few offers."

"What about Frank?"

"He left. He had jobs around here for a while, then our oldest brother, Patrick, found a job for him in Ballarat, so he left."

"What sort of work was he doing?"

"Patrick got him a job with some businessman in Ballarat. He was a driver for this man. I think he owned a pub or something. I was never really sure what the job really was. Frank wouldn't talk about it much."

"Where is Frank now?"

"I don't know. He just disappeared. Don't even know if he is alive. Just vanished. We never heard of him again. It was so unlike him. When he had days off he used to come home and see Mum. Mum struggled to bring up us kids and Frank never forgot it. He used to send Mum some money, never let Dad know. Dad had a problem with the pub and the ponies, Mum never had any money. Then one day it stopped.

For a while we weren't worried. Just thought he must have been away on a job somewhere, but then we started to worry. It was so unlike him not to contact Mum, or send her a few bob. Danny, one of my other brothers, and I decided to go into Ballarat and ask his boss where he was. Patrick, our eldest brother, was in Melbourne then. Anyway we found the pub, and his boss, but he said Frank had left town. It seemed strange but the boss said Frank had been in a bit of bother and decided it would be best to shoot through. That seemed so unlike Frank. It was more like Patrick, he was always in trouble, how he stayed out of jail I will never know. Anyway, that was it, the boss didn't know where he was, we didn't know and we never heard from him again. He just disappeared, it was so unlike him. I still miss him, he was my favourite brother, not that you should have favourites. He was such a gentle man, he wouldn't hurt anyone."

"Did the boss say anything else?"

"No, nothing."

"What did Frank do?"

"He was the boss's driver, did odd jobs, messages, ran people around town."

"Did you know the boss's name?"

"No. Frank just called him the boss. I think his name was Barry, or Jim, or something like that. It was so long ago. I know Frank wasn't really happy working there. One time when he came home he was upset. His boss had done the dirty on one of his partners and Frank didn't think it was right. He knew the man and reckoned he was a real good honest sort of bloke. Frank was like that, you treated people fair. I think he was thinking about leaving. Perhaps he did, but he would have told us, especially Mum."

"Who was the partner?"

"Oh, his family had a big hardware store in Ballarat. It was an unusual name, that's why I remember it. Foreign, but they had been here since the Gold Rushes. Kempner."

"Are they still in Ballarat?"

"No, the business went bust. There was some argument between Frank's boss and Kempner. Don't know what it was. It happened about six months before Frank disappeared. He was very upset."

"Are there any Kempners still in Ballarat?"

"No, they all left. I think they went to Melbourne."

It was approaching afternoon tea time in the Aged Hostel and I could see Dot had her eye on joining the other residents at the table, besides I thought I had learnt all that I was likely to learn. I thanked her for her time and made my farewell, leaving her with my phone number in case she remembered something else about her brother's disappearance.

Driving back to Melbourne I thought of Mrs Oliver and Merry's disappearance. Dot was another old lady grieving for a loved one. Their lives were so different yet both lived each day with the loss and uncertainty. All my hunch, and my investigation, had uncovered was another disappearance. No linkages. No leads. As a detective I had had no success. Perhaps I should give up?

Then there was Kempner. That seemed to be important to Ox. The business had folded and they had left town. Perhaps they had gone to Melbourne. There wouldn't be many people with that name. Perhaps I could try the phone book. I decided to have one last try. I wondered whether I was really looking for answers or just enjoying poking my nose into other people's business.

10 A BAD BUSINESS

Suzie

Next morning I commenced my search. It was not a very long search. As Dot had said it was an unusual name and there were only five listings in the telephone directory.

Melbourne would be a likely place for a businessman to try to rebuild his business. He would possibly have contacts in the city who could help him to re-establish his life.

The first two calls were unsuccessful. At the first there was no answer and the second brushed off my enquiry suspecting I was a marketer trying to sell some product or raise money for charity. I decided I needed a story. It had worked for Dot yesterday, although I thought Dot just enjoyed having someone new to talk to and would not have been concerned if I was a Martian. Today my story would be I was researching Ballarat businesses for a history project on old Ballarat families. I hoped that would give me access to a Kempner.

My third try was more helpful. I spoke with a woman who informed me her husband's family used to be in Ballarat many years earlier. She didn't know the details but her husband might be able to help. I arranged to phone back later when her husband finished his shift at the factory. After speaking with him it was agreed that we meet that afternoon. The traffic was heavy with the peak hour rush of workers heading home as I drove out to Melton.

I guessed Michael Kempner would be in his early forties. His blonde wife a few years younger. There were three children ranging from six upwards. The oldest a teenager from the look of her clothes.

I explained my cover story and asked if his family were involved in hardware in Ballarat. He told me his father's family once owned a large hardware store there, but had sold it many years earlier. While he was born in Ballarat the family had moved to Melbourne not long after his birth so he really did not know anything about the business. It had been a family business. The family story was that his great, great, great, something, grandfather—his name was Henri Phillipe, the same as his father—was a young man exploring the world and had arrived in Australia as crew on a sailing ship but had jumped ship and gone to the goldfields like so many others. However he had quickly decided that he could do better trading in shovels than digging for gold. That had led to him setting up a shop in a tent. Then he had opened a store selling other goods to miners and over the years it had grown into a large hardware business. His father was the youngest of five boys who had all been involved in the business. Apparently it had once been a good business but then had deteriorated. He gathered there must have been some tensions over the business because of ill feelings within the family although the subject was never discussed. He thought there was a falling out between the older brothers, who wanted to continue the business as it was, and his father who could see competition problems coming and wanted to modernise the business. His brothers refused so his father had gone into a second business with another man.

"What was it?"

"Apparently there was this young bloke around town who was thought of as a businessman who would go places. Dad reckoned that if he went into business with him and put up some money he would do well. It would give him another income if the hardware went the way he thought it would. It didn't work out. I understand the new business went bad and Dad lost all his money. He had borrowed heavily. As well the hardware business went bad, as Dad expected it would, and he lost the lot. The family had to sell up. The other brothers were OK but Dad had this other business and borrowings and he lost everything."

"Do you know what the other business was?"

"No. Dad would not talk about it but I think it might have been a pub. I know he was very angry with his partner. He felt he had been cheated. He came to Melbourne and got a job in a warehouse handling industrial products but he was never happy."

"Did he say who the partner was?"

"No, but sometimes after a few drinks he would get really upset and he would swear 'he would get even with that bloody swindling Bernie James!' I don't know who Bernie James was but I suspected it was the partner who had cheated him."

"Did he ever get even?"

"Not that I know of. Dad would never talk about it but I think he was frightened. He once said the partner arranged for some heavies to visit him and get him to sign some papers. I guess it must have been to do with the business."

"What were they like?"

"I don't know. I think there were two from the way he spoke. Dad once said something about the dwarf and his mate. Dad reckoned the little bloke was the nasty one. The big man wasn't so bad. It was almost like he didn't want to be there."

"Did he ever mention the name of the partner?"

"No. One day he saw him on the television. He had become an important businessman. Dad went right off his head. I think he went to the police or newspapers or something. I was only a little kid. Anyway two men came and picked him up and bashed him. After that he was very scared and would never talk about it unless he was drunk."

"Were they the same men?"

"I don't think so. I remember once Dad was talking to a mate and he said one bloke was a thug but the other was younger and very expensively dressed. He was the frightening one who did most of the bashing. The thug just held Dad while the younger man really went to work on him. Dad reckoned he got a kick out of hurting people. He was a psycho!"

"Did he ever find out who he was?"

"Not that I know of, but Dad was sure his ex-partner was behind it."

"Did your father ever say anything else about the men or his partner?"

"I don't remember. I think I would have been only four or five at the time. Most of it is things that have been said much later. Oh, Dad did say they drove a very fancy car, one of those imported Italian things. Don't know what it was."

"Is your father alive now?"

"No, he died about ten years ago. I think the experience in Ballarat really shook him up. He never really got over it. He got jobs here in Melbourne but he was never happy."

It appeared that my search for the elusive Ballarat business man of the Grande Imperial might be Bernie James. That was probably Dot O'Hartigan's 'Barry' or 'Jim'. I still didn't have any reason to explain my dread standing outside the hotel or a link to Merry. From the story the Boss appeared to have a reputation for using violence, and the description of the younger man was of a man that I did not ever want to meet.

"Arthur Belmond might know."

"Who is Arthur Belmond?"

"He used to work for Dad. They used to be good friends but then they sort of drifted apart."

"Do you have any contact details for him?"

"Yes. He lives out in the Dandenong Ranges, near Belgrave. I should have his address and phone number somewhere. He used to be Dad's accountant in Ballarat so he may know some of the history."

The thought of violent thugs made me think very seriously about asking any more questions. I seemed to be on the edge of something very unpleasant. It was not what I wanted. The thought of spending time with my grandson and walking in a park with him was much more appealing than meeting up with some violent psycho. I decided to end my enquiries.

11 ARTHUR BELMOND

Suzie

When I woke next morning I had a change of mind. I decided I would give it one more try.

So far my enquiries had not found any answers. In fact rather than solving the mystery of what happened to Merry, I now had another missing person with 'the Ox', some dubious gambling activity and a falling out between business partners. Plus a car crash. None of it seemed to have any connection to Merry. Nor could I see how any of it would be connected.

Perhaps Phillip Kempner's friend could help. It was a lovely day, the sun was shining and the sky a clear cloudless blue. I always enjoyed the Dandenong Ranges, and if my enquiries were fruitless I could always find a nice coffee shop and then wander one of the local gardens open for public visits.

It wasn't hard to find the address of Arthur Belmond. The drive along the freeway and Ferntree Gully Road had been easy as all the morning traffic was heading in the opposite direction. At Belgrave I turned into Old Monbulk Road and started to look for the number Michael Kempner had given me. As I passed the Puffing Billy Steam Railway station I had a sudden memory of my parents taking me on the little train one weekend break away from boarding school. The tiny train always brought smiles to the faces of passengers and passers-by. One day, when he is a few years older, I must bring little Charlie for a ride. I was sure he and his parents would enjoy the trip. A little further along the winding road I found the address Michael Kempner had given me. I didn't even need to use the GPS.

Like so many others in the area the house was tucked away down a long driveway and hidden amid the trees and shrubs of a large garden. When I pressed the bell on the white painted weatherboard wall I heard a few bars of the 'Hallelujah Chorus' come from inside the house. Then the barking of a small dog. The door opened and a smiling rotund balding man stood in front of me. He was younger than I expected. Probably of similar age to myself. For some reason I had expected an older man, perhaps because I associated him with the Ox, or Dot, or even Phillip Kempner who was dead.

I introduced myself and began with my story about researching Ballarat business history. I thought I was becoming quite proficient with my little white lie.

Arthur was agreeable to my questioning and invited me into the kitchen.

While his wife poured cups of tea for us, he explained his background. He was born and raised in Ballarat, after finishing school he had been able to get a job in the accounts section of Kempner's hardware business. It was a very solid business in those days. Because his parents didn't have much money it was necessary for him to work and then study at night and part-time. He was able to do accountancy that way. Eventually he became the accountant for Kempner's.

He had a great working arrangement with Phillip Kempner who was the brother in charge of the finances. The business was a family business with five brothers involved.

Rather than go immediately to the threats and the bashing I decided to let Arthur talk a little more about himself and the business. As Kempner's son had told me, the business, while thriving, faced some challenges. Belmond recalled that as the profits grew the family kept increasing their drawings to cover their increasing lifestyle demands and not re-investing in the business, then, when it became necessary to invest they borrowed money. Phillip Kempner saw the risk but was overruled by his brothers who wanted to keep up their lifestyles.

One day at work Phillip told Arthur he had decided to go into a second business with a partner. He had mortgaged his house and invested the money with a man called Bernie James. He was a young man that was going to go places. The investment was in a hotel. Arthur had heard stories of this Bernie James and was cautious about any dealings with him; there were whispers among his accounting friends, but Kempner did not take any notice.

"That was when everything fell apart. A big national company opened in competition to Kempner's hardware. They could buy goods at better prices and sell for a lower margin, sometimes even at cost. Kempner's profits collapsed as Phillip had expected but the family still drew the same amount from the business. Some families were like that.

Eventually the bank refused any more funds and the business had to close. All that was left was the real estate but most of that went to cover debts. At the same time there was a falling out between Kempner and James. Apparently Kempner thought the business was making good profits and should pay a dividend but James reckoned it wasn't. He claimed it was losing money. Kempner asked me to look at the books and they were a bit suspicious. I felt some of the cash was not properly accounted for. That led to another argument between Phillip and Bernie James. Phillip wanted out but James would not return the money. He reckoned he didn't have any. Eventually I understood the agreement was that James would return some of the money and the rest later if the business 'came good'. From what Phillip told me it never did. After a while Phillip moved to Melbourne and got a job. I also came here and found a job with an engineering works. It worked well for me, eventually I became Chief Financial Officer for the company."

"What happened with Kempner?"

"Phillip wasn't so fortunate. He had various jobs. None of them seemed to lead anywhere. I think he had a problem changing from being the boss to becoming an employee."

"His son told me that he had some other dealing with James. Something about being threatened."

The look in Belmond's face changed. A worried look replaced the smiles. "What do you know?"

From the tone of his voice I got the strong impression that it was a subject that I needed to approach carefully.

"His son said that he had recognised James from the television, however he now had a different name. He was also now very wealthy and Kempner approached him about the balance of the money".

"I don't think there is any benefit in going over old issues. They are all history."

"His son also said that his father was threatened and bashed very badly by some thugs?"

"It wasn't only Phillip. They bashed me too!"

"Who was it? Why?"

"To keep us quiet. Phillip knew James' new name. He never told me who it was but that didn't stop them from attacking me. I think they also threatened to harm Phillip's family. He was very frightened and never discussed the subject again."

"Did he ever say who it was? Was it a very big man?"

"No, Phillip only said that there were two of them. I don't know if it was the same ones who bashed me but it could have been. Three men came here. Two men who looked like muscle, you know the sort that work out in gyms, and the third man was younger. He was the boss. He gave the orders, the others just did what they were told. The young one was nasty. Really nasty. I think he enjoyed hurting people. He was a flash dresser as well: fancy shoes and gold chains."

"Why did they bash you?"

"I think it must have been because I could back up Phillip's story. I knew what the arrangements were because Phillip had shown me some letters and I had checked out the books—such as they were."

"Did you ever find out who was behind the attacks?"

"No. I didn't want to go there. Nor did Phillip. I spent a week in hospital after the bashing. They kidnapped me for two days. My wife was frantic."

"Did you report it to the police?"

"No. They had warned me not to go to the police or I would have an accident. I just said I had fallen out of a tree in the garden. I was really scared."

"And you have no idea who it was?"

"No, it must have had something to do with Bernie James. There was no other reason. They just said never to discuss anything with Kempner. And don't ask questions! I certainly don't ever want to see that young one again. I think he was mad. He liked to hurt people."

I made my farewell to the Belmonds and drove to Olinda and found a coffee shop to mull over the new information. It would seem that the Grande Imperial was at the centre of some very unpleasant business. Perhaps that explained the feeling Merry and I had had when we were there, and again when Peter and I had visited. It still had no connection to Merry's disappearance.

I decided to visit Cloudehill. It was always one of my favourite gardens. Regardless of the time of the year there was always something beautiful to see. While it was still too early for the leaves of the weeping maples and the beeches to show their magnificent colours, the perennial borders were still making a fine display. I wandered the garden admiring the various rooms and walks. As beautiful as they were my mind kept returning to my visits to Phillip Kempner's son and Arthur Belmond. The image of a vicious young man kept recurring no matter how beautiful the trees and plants looked. I decided I would ring Roley Donaldson again and discuss my new information. However I would leave it until later in the day, after he had probably made plans for the evening. I didn't want to make excuses to turn down the invitation I expected.

It was eight thirty when I called Roley. I was sure he would have his night organised by then. I told him of my various visits and the stories of the bashings. He listened with interest before replying.

He remembered the big man at the hotel, he assumed he was security of some sort. There would have been lots of cash changing hands. Apart from that he had no knowledge of him.

He had heard of some partner in the hotel but it was before his time.

He had never heard of any Kempner or Belmond.

He knew nothing of any bashings, or violence, but from the sound of it, perhaps it might be best not to enquire too closely. Sometimes there could be unpleasant business behind such happenings. It would be wise to stay well away and not become involved.

As expected he offered an invitation to a quiet dinner the following week—two days before he was due to return to Thailand. I had enjoyed my lunch with Roley, and I was sure a dinner date with him would be fun, but I decided that I didn't need the possible complications it may involve. I made my excuse that I was committed to baby-sit my grandson again and sadly could not accept.

After I had hung up on Roley I had to admit to myself that my amateur detective work had brought me no closer to solving Merry's disappearance. Perhaps I would be better concentrating on my roses and my grandson.

Then I thought of Peter. Would I have turned down an invitation from him? But then he was in Sydney, and I was in Melbourne.

12 PETER'S MATE'S MATE

Peter

Flying back to Sydney I wondered if it would be like the last time I saw Suzie. One day she was there, the next she had disappeared never to be seen again for forty years. I had no address, only a phone number and an email address. Even that I didn't fully understand. I had known her as Sue but she was now Suzie. Mrs Oliver had referred to her as Susan. Her email was susanf25. I had known her as Sue Benedict. She had mentioned an ex-husband but not much more. No indication of when, or where or why. It would seem she was probably using her married name. All I knew was she had two children somewhere in Melbourne. While we had chatted over meals, and during our car and our train trips as well as during our stay at Oakleigh, I still knew little of her private life. She had spoken freely of her thoughts and views but little of her past. I had no idea if she still worked. Probably not since her time seemed to be her own. I didn't even know very much about what sort of work she did, or used to do. In the time we had spent together she had spoken very little of herself. I gathered she was interested in fashion from our first meeting and obviously she was a keen gardener from the plants she had bought in Ballarat. I knew her views on many subjects but none of her history since I had last known her.

She had dropped me off at my friends' house in Glen Iris. They had been out when we arrived. I had the key to the house and yet somehow it didn't feel right to ask her in. We stood in the street making small talk, both feeling uncomfortable, unlike earlier in the day. We had almost parted without even exchanging phone numbers. I had no idea where she lived and sitting in the plane I realised I didn't even know if she called herself by her maiden name of Benedict or used her ex-husband's name. I still thought of her by the maiden name that I knew her by when we were in London. Yet somehow I felt we had become very close during our trip to the Western District and our two trips to Ballarat. It was a strange feeling of somehow being connected as more than friends, yet still knowing so little of what had passed in each other's lives. We didn't even know if we would ever see each other again. Did I want to see her? I certainly found her great company and she had lost none of the appeal that I had found so attractive all those years ago. Indeed she had matured beautifully. I wished I had.

Sydney airport was, as usual, in chaos with rebuilding work. I went down to the train station and caught the underground train into the city, then changed to an express bus at Wynyard. Fortunately the bus was only part filled and I missed the crush of peak hour workers heading home. Crossing the Harbour Bridge on the bus I had only a quick view of the harbour that is the great beauty of Sydney, unlike the endless suburbs that spread to the south and out and up into the Blue Mountains to the west. At Avalon I found a taxi to take me back to our house overlooking Pitt Water.

Claire and I loved the house overlooking the waterway that is so beloved by yachties and boaties. In the inlet below our house the yachts rocked quietly on their moorings in the late afternoon light as the sun cast its last shadows across the ripples of the water. After living with me in so many mining camps the attraction of a permanent base overlooking water had proved irresistible for Claire. We had made it our home when I became a fly in/fly out manager and eventually I used it as a base for my consulting work with newly established mines. The view from the house was one we enjoyed every day that we had lived there.

Now without Claire it was a bit big and felt empty. The house and garden were the same but somehow lacked the life that Claire had given them. Especially the garden which she had created with her favourite native plants. I had grown up in inner city Sydney, but having spent many years at mine sites far from cities and towns, had come to enjoy the space, the view of the water and the bush around us. It was an easy five minute drive to the beach if I wanted to swim or surf and easy to get to the airport if I needed to fly anywhere. It held so many memories of Claire, memories that would no longer increase in number.

In our first years together Claire had moved with me from one mine to another. The mines always seem to be in hot dry climates, hot wet climates or cold wet climates, and always remote. Perhaps not all mines are like that but the ones we worked in certainly were. Regardless of the conditions, she had adapted and made the best of it. It was that characteristic that had first attracted me to her in South Africa and it made our early years so much better. After our son was born and education became important we made the decision to find a permanent base. We had finally decided on two possibilities. One was the house we eventually bought; the other option was a house in the Blue Mountains over-looking the Jamison Valley. The name had seemed almost appropriate and the view was superb. As well I had a very good friend, Ernie Young, who lived nearby. Like me he was also in the mining industry and we had frequently worked together on projects. In the end the view of water triumphed but we always had an open invitation to visit Ernie and his wife at Leura. Their home was one of Claire's and my favourite places.

The years that followed became the hardest period of our life together. I would be away for long periods of time and Claire would have all the day to day responsibilities of the family. She had her activities and friends and then I would return and interfere with her life, upset the running of the house, and disappear back to work. For me it was not a satisfying life either. I didn't enjoy being a part-time husband, or missing so much of the growing-up of our child. The stresses had almost broken our marriage. Fortunately, unlike some of my workmates, we held together through that hard time and remained married, but it was the worst and most difficult period of our lives. Eventually when I became a consultant and worked from home we regained our lives and our relationship recovered. Those final years until Claire became sick had been our best years, although we had both had to adjust. Claire still had her garden and her groups. I had never been a sporting person and spending three days a week on the golf course or bowling-green held no appeal. Living alone in mining camps workers often filled in their time with drinking, gambling or reading. When alcohol testing with zero levels had become a condition of entry to mine-sites drinking was no longer possible, not that I was ever a great drinker. I don't know if it was my nature, or the upbringing my parents had given me, but gambling had never been an interest. I read. Anything and everything. I finally found another interest that gave Claire her own time and space and got me out of the house. I took up building working miniature models of early steam engines and steam trains. I loved the challenge in researching the details and then creating them in the workshop in my shed.

Thinking about Claire and Suzie at the same time made me feel uncomfortable. It felt like a betrayal of Claire to think of another woman. Especially in our home which held so many memories. I wondered how Claire would feel. She had discussed the possibility before she died and she had told me not to worry if I met someone, but I had not really believed her, or that it might happen. Perhaps I was just a lonely old man who needed company, and Suzie had certainly provided that. A dog would be an easier solution.

I was very surprised when Suzie rang and informed me of her trip to Ballarat. She told me the news of her enquiries. I think she was rather enjoying her sleuthing although she hadn't come up with any answers. Only another disappearance and what appeared to be some dubious business practices. The story of Kempner being bashed was certainly unpleasant but it was so long ago and didn't involve Suzie, or any part of her life. It would hardly put her at risk, and besides, she was giving up on any further enquiries so it was not a worry.

I had unsettled feelings. I was pleased to hear from her again and looked forward to keeping in touch, but still didn't know whether she would phone me again or if I should call her.

Every two years there is a get together of past and present workers associated with one of the Pilbara iron ore mines in Western Australia. At one time I had worked there when jobs in my particular field were difficult to find. Some years it is fifty people, other years there could be several hundred. It varies according to who is off roster, retired or looking for a job. Groups form and change as old mates meet up. Managers drift into groups, the blasters relive past mistakes, the truckies cart more and more ore and the office workers huddle in the corner. The gossip goes on. "Don't take a job there, it will be closed in six months", "The bosses are a bunch of bastards", "They're opening a new mine next to BHP's and I reckon you should be able to get a job, see Bruce".

I decided to go for the afternoon session. It was in the Beer Garden at the usual pub. When I turned up it was in full swing. Already I could see that by the end of the night some old grudges would resurface and the bouncers would have a busy night with a few drunken miners. Most of the men and the few women who came I wouldn't know, but there was always someone I had worked with who would turn up and we would talk old times and more recent happenings. This year it was Wayne.

Wayne had been a young lad when I first came across him in a New Guinea copper mine. He was a great operator. He had the ability to get on with anyone, do any job and be content with the camp. He quickly got shifted from driving trucks to being the fix-it man for any problems. He worked hard in the bush and played hard in the city on his time off.

That sort of work and lifestyle was hard on relationships and Wayne's behaviour certainly didn't help. Every time I met him there was a new past relationship. He would always tell me that he had learnt from experience and the next one would be the one. I had heard that story many times over the years.

I mentioned to him that I had just been to Ballarat looking at its gold mining history. Wayne said he knew an old King's Cross character who had worked in Ballarat years ago, and sometimes talked of his experiences there. He wasn't mining in those days but worked for some hotel. It was all very dodgy from some of the stories he used to tell. Wayne had come across him because the old character used to work in the mines when he was broke, which seemed to happen frequently. Slowgo, as he was called, once worked for the owner of the hotel as a heavy collecting gambling debts. He would never say who the owner was, he just called him the Boss, but said you'd sometimes see him on TV. Apparently he had become a 'bigwig' business man these days. "All very important now" according to Slowgo.

Most jobs were just a visit with a mate but occasionally in difficult cases he had to pick up a kid, a wife, or girlfriend until the debt was paid. They never complained to the police after they were released because their husband or father or boyfriend was involved in illegal gambling. Occasionally the debtor was roughed up, but usually the threat was enough. I suddenly got very interested. It could have been the explanation of our young girl that disappeared and reappeared. Another time he and a mate picked up a girl in Melbourne and took her to Ballarat—not the hotel but a building across the road from it. Next morning he was paid off, given some cash for expenses and a briefcase, and told to return to Melbourne, catch 'The Spirit of Progress' to Sydney that night and deliver the case to a man in King's Cross next morning.

He did as he was told. Discovered he liked King's Cross, lost his pay and a week of his life to the booze and the girls, quit his old job and never went back to Melbourne or Ballarat. From then on it was the Cross or the mines. Never heard anything more of what happened in Ballarat. Assumed she was released like the other ones when the debt was paid. Never saw or heard of his accomplice again.

Did the story have something to do with Merry? When did this all happen? I decided I needed to meet Wayne's mate.

13 FINDING THE CHARACTER

Peter

Finding Slowgo wasn't hard. Wayne had told me he would be very easy to find. He was well known all around King's Cross as befitted somebody who had spent most of his life—and money—there.

Wayne hadn't told me which pub but said I would find him in one after midday.

He frequented three or four around the Cross, depending on which publicans he had annoyed recently and which ones had banned him.

If he was on 'holidays' he would be down at one of the pubs that old time wharfies used to support, especially on pay day, when the pubs had topless barmaids.

I reckoned he wouldn't be hard to locate.

There were various ideas about how he had got his name. Some said it was because every horse he put his money on would go slow. Others said that it was his advice to mates on developing intimate relationships with women, but nobody had ever seen any signs of great success in that department either. There were even those who said it was the way he worked but they weren't sure because nobody had ever seen him work.

I reckoned he would avoid the big brash pubs with loud music and discos that attracted the crowds at night, so I decided to start on the old corner pubs away from Macleay Street.

When Wayne told the story of him working as a standover man I had formed a picture of a large, thickset man with big muscles. Wayne's description had been different to my preconception.

I had no joy at the first, but at the second pub there was a skinny man, with thin grey hair and a weathered face showing the effects of the daily consumption of large amounts of beer, that seemed to fit Wayne's description, including the tattoo of a dancing island lady with a deep scar across her torso. Wayne had told me the story of how Slowgo had had an accident on a mine-site and his arm had been badly slashed. Apparently Slowgo preferred to tell a story of how he got the scar in a knife fight in the Philippines. Wayne had warned me Slowgo liked to embellish his stories.

He was sitting on what I supposed was his personal stool in the corner of the little side bar, next to what had once been the Ladies Lounge and was now called the Gaming Room. Age and hard living had taken its toll on him. He looked as if he could use a good feed rather than another beer.

I decided to heed the advice of his name and go slow. I nodded to him, ordered a beer, but waited to let him open the conversation. When I was on my second pot he started to chat. Firstly it was the weather, then the quality of the beer before moving on to the character of the barman who apparently could be very abrupt.

I learnt that he liked the horses and the girls. "Two very expensive hobbies."

He told me that when his luck turned bad he would go off and find work in some mine to get a new kitty together. That was obviously where Wayne had come across him. Wayne also had a reputation for fast women and slow horses so they would have had lots to talk about. I told him I used to work in mines myself and chatted about various mines. It seemed we had never worked on the same sites. I dropped Wayne's name and asked if he had ever come across him. He recognised the name and told of working with him. I hoped that having a mutual friend might make him a bit more open in his conversation.

I mentioned I had been to the races in Ballarat recently and he told me he had once worked there.

His boss had run a pub there. He was the big man of the local SP bookies and he used to run invitation only gambling nights for selected people. This was where the Boss got his cash to finance the start of a successful real estate development. When I asked who his Ballarat employer was he suddenly became very unhelpful. I got the impression that he reckoned that even today it would be unwise to talk too much about the Boss, or to upset him.

Sensing there were some things he didn't want to discuss I changed the subject and bought him another beer. As the beers came and went he talked more and more of his life. He was one of those lonely characters whose only company is the person on the barstool beside them. Not all his stays in mining camps were due to the need of new funds.

Sometimes it had been advisable to depart the Cross for other reasons. Debts and jealous boyfriends had played their part. I found it hard to imagine Slowgo as the answer to a woman's desire but then maybe I am not the best judge. Perhaps in his youth he had been more handsome. Sometimes the police had prompted a quick departure. He had certainly had a colourful life in a dingy sort of way.

Getting any useful information from him was difficult. When he was sober he was very voluble on his pet subjects but very circumspect on several questions that I asked him. When he was drunk he was very talkative but it was difficult to make much sense of some of his comments. There was about five minutes between the two states when I thought he had loosened up and might say something unguarded but he didn't. Perhaps he would have talked more openly to an old drinking partner from his past but he certainly wasn't going to say too much to a stranger he had just met.

Every now and again I would return to the hotel in Ballarat. Did he work in the bar or was he a cook? Did he ever get involved with the gambling? From his answers he was neither. He was the Boss's offsider. He wasn't allowed to gamble but he did pick up and drop of a few guests. Sometimes he had to help them. I gathered from his comments that there was more involved with the help than just driving a few drunks home. Then he would get edgy as if my questions were entering bad territory and I would quickly change the subject.

Finally I decided I would have to bring up the girl who disappeared and reappeared, and Merry's disappearance. From the way the beers kept disappearing if I didn't do it soon he would be beyond words. I started with the girl who had reappeared. I hoped that it would be old history and not threatening. He admitted that one of his jobs was to babysit a few people and occasionally he and a mate would have to help people find some money but no one was ever seriously hurt. Not that his mate was much help. He was a bit slow, not retarded, but just slow. He was big, really big, which sometimes helped. People would look at him and not argue. Locals used to joke about "the long and short of it" and say, "Here comes the Giant and the Dwarf". I got the feeling that it annoyed Slowgo to be thought of as short. He was average size, maybe shrunken a little with age but probably never the Adonis that he was in his own mind.

When I asked if he had ever babysat a girl from Melbourne he went very quiet. He may have been very drunk but the look on his face and his answer didn't match. He had never had anything to do with Melbourne. That was the end of our conversation. I got the impression I had gone too far. It was obvious he thought some things in his past were best not remembered, and definitely best not discussed.

The way he kept changing the subject whenever I had asked about his Ballarat boss increased my curiosity. Although it was obvious he hadn't worked for him for years he still referred to him as 'The Boss'. The Boss was certainly interesting, and Slowgo's comments to Wayne and the way he shut up when I raised the question of a Melbourne girl was very suspicious. Certainly there would have been criminal behaviour but there was nothing to make a definite connection to Suzie's missing friend. Yet for some reason I felt there was a connection.

I decided to email Suzie with news of my afternoon and make the suggestion that I return to Melbourne and we take another trip to Ballarat. Meanwhile she could use her Melbourne business connections to find out who had once been involved with the hotel and then gone into real estate development. I thought of phoning her but decided that maybe an email would be better.

I wasn't sure whether it was enquires about Ballarat that were important, or if it was the chance to see her again.

Little did I know that next morning when Slowgo sobered up he reckoned that it would be a good idea to let the publican Red Phil know that someone had been making enquires about his Melbourne mate, the Boss, and Ballarat. He reckoned the information should be worth a couple of bottles of rum.

Little did I know a bottle of rum would cause so much pain for Suzie and me!

14 THE ACCIDENT

Suzie

I called Peter from the hospital.

I had had a lovely night at Max and Amelia's. It was always great to have the time alone with my grandson, and I had enjoyed babysitting while they had spent a wonderful evening celebrating a friend's thirtieth birthday at a restaurant in Prahran.

They asked me to stay the night but I wanted to go home. I hoped to finish some planting in my garden next day and I knew that if I stayed I would end up playing with young Charles after breakfast and never make it home before midday. At that time of night there wouldn't be much traffic on the road and it would be a quick trip, much quicker than in the daytime traffic next morning.

Coming off the freeway I noticed lights in my rear vision mirror. From their height it had to be a truck and it was moving very fast. I was on the speed limit and it was gaining on me rapidly. The lights in my rear view mirror started to dazzle me yet the driver of the truck made no effort to lower the beam. It came right up behind me and tailgated me. The cabin of my car seemed to be so full of light it was hard to see the road ahead through the front window. I planted my foot to accelerate away but the truck sped up as well. Still it was right behind me. Looking at the speedo I saw I was doing one hundred and twenty, way over the limit, and not wise for that road. I took my foot of the accelerator and started to slow. The truck bumped me, pulled back and then bumped me a second time. I became really angry and then scared. I flattened the accelerator to the floor and pulled away from my assailant. Again the truck accelerated and started to overtake me. Suddenly when it was level with me it swerved towards me. I moved to the edge of the road but he just kept moving in towards me. All I could see was the big wheel of the truck coming closer and closer to me. I hit the brakes but so did the truck and it still remained alongside me. I tried to accelerate away again but so did the truck, still it was beside me. As we came to a bend in the road it pulled in even closer and instinctively I moved away from that big spinning tyre. I felt my off wheels leave the asphalt and bump along the gravel verge. Still the truck was pulling in towards me, pushing me further off the road. As the car went through the drain I could feel it start to roll but somehow it stopped and righted itself. The trees in front of me were rushing up. I was sure that I would hit one of the many gum trees along that section of the road but fortunately between the brakes and some shrubby bushes the car stopped a metre from the trunk of a massive red gum. I was sitting there shaking when a man ran up. He had been following behind and seen me go off the road. He was sure I would be dead. He got me out and called the ambulance and police.

The ambulance arrived first. Not that I needed much attention. Mostly it was shock and a small scratch on my forehead. Nevertheless they insisted I go to hospital for observation. I told them I was fine, no problems. I just wanted to go home. My beautiful yellow car sat surrounded by broken shrubs, its grill, bonnet and side panels wrecked. One wheel was buckled and the airbags had discharged. There was no way I could drive it home. That was when I realised I was shaking and I had to agree it might be best to spend a night in the hospital.

Then the police arrived. They didn't seem to believe my story. I had the very strong feeling that they thought it was an overwrought woman who had been drinking and was driving too fast. I had had one glass of wine with dinner but even my breath test didn't change their attitude. They had no interest in my description of the white truck and by then my rescuer had left so there was no one to confirm my story. All there was were my wheel tracks leaving the road. The truck had left no marks on the asphalt.

"Did you see the truck?" The concern in Peter's voice was obvious.

"I saw the lights. I couldn't see the truck. I remember looking out the side window and all I could see was the front wheel. It was a white truck. I didn't see anything else. Only the wheel and the front of the truck coming towards me. There was a scratch on the mudguard, a deep long brown scratch, and a strange smell."

My rescuer had told me it was a white tip truck. It stopped when I left the road and then drove off very fast when he had driven up.

"Who knew you would be on the road that night?"

"The kids. I'd arranged to babysit for them. I guess their

friends would have known I was there but they wouldn't know if I was going home or staying overnight."

"Could it have been an accident? Road rage?"

"No, Peter! He wanted to put me off the road. It was deliberate."

Peter offered to fly down immediately. This time I wanted him to have my address.

When I got home from hospital there was a voice message on my phone.

"Stop asking questions!"

I waited for Peter.

15 WHY

Peter

Suzie was pleased to see me. I liked the thought of that.

She was bruised and had a few cuts and scrapes but no serious injuries. She was still shaky when she spoke of the crash and angry about the damage to her beloved car. Fortunately the car hadn't rolled, and when she told me how close she had come to the trees along the side of the road, I felt so grateful that she was OK. Scrubby bush had slowed the car down and she had managed to stop in time. One metre more and she would have hit a big tree. Then it would have been a very different story. A few kilometres further along the road and she could have gone over a cliff.

She had already worked out that this was no ordinary accident. Someone had deliberately wanted to push her off the road in a place where she would probably be killed. And they knew where to find her, and what she was doing. Suzie had already realised she was in danger.

I felt very guilty. Somehow all this had started when I had reappeared on the scene. I had to agree with her, whoever it was had wanted to, at the very least, seriously harm her and quite possibly kill her.

Yet I knew of no reason why I could bring on trouble for another person. My life was uncomplicated. No financial problems, no jealous husbands or ex-girlfriends. No dubious business dealings. I was boring! Well not to me, I enjoyed life, but nothing I did should bring death threats to someone I hardly knew. It must be Suzie.

"Do you have enemies?"

"Of course not!"

"What about husbands, boyfriends, business partners?"

"My ex-husband I haven't seen for years. Besides, believe me he is happy with his latest bimbo. I should be the one causing him grief but I don't. I was glad to see him go. No boyfriends and no business problems. No fights with the neighbours. Nothing. No threats until you came along."

"Well it can't be me. I've never had this sort of problem until you came into my life."

"Well, nor have I until I met you again!"

If she is right then it must be something one, or both of us, have done or said since we have met at the gallery in Melbourne. But what? We took a trip to Ballarat sightseeing. We visited her friends in the country and we went back to Ballarat. Sightseeing seemed innocuous. Her friends were hardly threating violent types and even the second trip to Ballarat had led nowhere. The only questions that had come up were where was Billy going, and why, and where was Merry, and why had she disappeared? Perhaps they were the questions someone didn't want answered. But why now? That was so long ago. Who would be worried by such questions? Perhaps her questions to Kempner and Belmond had been the cause of her trouble. However they seemed unlikely to talk to anyone. They wanted to avoid any trouble.

Even then why attack Suzie? Perhaps it was really directed only at her and had nothing to do with me. Is she being honest with me, or is there something in her background that she is not telling me? It seems unlikely from the girl I once knew, but that was many years ago. We all change.

It was made to look like an accident. An accident that would not lead to questions being asked if she were killed, and yet would frighten off a normal person if she survived. A shooting would lead to investigations and that was probably something whoever was behind it all would want to avoid. Whoever it was certainly did not like questions being asked.

The only link seemed to be Ballarat. Was it something we had said or done in Ballarat? Perhaps it was questions about Ballarat? In Sydney I had spoken with Wayne, but only about the gossip around the gambling. He had provided the details so it seemed unlikely he had any concerns. Slowgo was different. He obviously had things to hide but then he didn't know my name. I had introduced myself as Peter and I don't think I ever mentioned my surname or where I lived. I suppose he could have tracked me down through Wayne but that also seemed unlikely, besides neither of them would know anything of Suzie. I had never mentioned her. I doubted they were linked to her accident. After all, if it was my asking questions why threaten Suzie? Why would anyone want to get at me through someone I barely knew, and who lived far away in Melbourne? If it was me why not just arrange an accident for me in Sydney? It wouldn't be that hard, a mugging in the street, a drive-by shooting. It seemed to happen all the time these days.

"Who have you told about your trip to Ballarat with me?" I asked.

"Ian, and of course Roley."

"Did you tell them about your second trip and your enquiries?"

"No, I haven't spoken to Ian, apart from that first time. I only saw Roley once although I did phone him after my last trip."

"Do you think they may have any reason to be concerned?"

"No. I've known Ian for years, from before he married Elizabeth, and he is very above board. Roley is a bit more dubious in his friends but he is harmless."

"It could be mistaken identity. The accident may have been meant for someone else."

"Someone with a yellow car, driving home late at night from her son's house! They have my phone number so they know where I live. That's a fair bit of mistaken identity! They knew where to find me so they must have been watching and still decided a grey-haired lady was their target."

I hadn't paid much attention to the grey hair. In fact I hadn't even seen it. Suzie's hairdresser had done a great job keeping the greys out of sight but I had to admit she was right. It seemed far too unlikely to be the wrong person unless some bad guys' communications had gone very badly awry.

"Who knew you were out that night?"

"Only Max and Amelia. Perhaps they had told their friends I was babysitting Charles."

Someone knew exactly what she was doing and when she would be on the road. So she must have been watched. They certainly knew her son's address and her phone number. I didn't even know where she lived until she phoned me after the accident. They must have been waiting for an opportunity to attack her so there would have to be more than one involved. You would hardly do surveillance in a big white truck.

"Have you seen anyone hanging around, watching your movements?"

"You think I was being watched?"

"Well someone knew you would be on the road that night. If it wasn't an accident then they must have been watching you."

"Peter, it wasn't an accident! Someone tried to kill me!"

"What about the phone call? When did you get it?"

"I know it wasn't on my answering machine when I left to go to Max's in the afternoon. I saw it when I came home from hospital. That was after I had phoned you from the hospital. It's still on the machine."

We checked the message again. It was a man's voice but it could have been anyone. There was no particular accent or anything to give a lead. Since Suzie had made a number of calls there was no possibility of calling the number back, not that I thought a thug would be stupid enough to make threatening calls on phones that could be traced. Perhaps the phone account would show a number but I thought it unlikely to be of any use. Besides you would hardly phone someone and leave a message and then try to run that person off the road. It was more probable that the call was made after the car crash. Someone must have been watching and knew she was still alive. That made sense. They knew she was still alive and so they called and left the warning message.

"Did you see anyone suspicious when you had the crash?"

"I was very shaken. It all seemed unreal. The ambulance arrived, then the police. There were a few others who stopped and watched for a while but I didn't pay any attention to them. It wasn't important. Of course there was my Good Samaritan who phoned for the ambulance."

"Did you get his name?"

"No. He waited until the ambulance arrived and then left."

The Good Samaritan was unlikely. If you have just been involved in a possible murder you would hardly call the police or ambulance. The police may have arrived before the ambulance and if you were involved you would not want to be at the crime site to become a witness. Probably he was innocent and felt he had done all he could and left. Maybe one of the other bystanders could have been connected with the truck and stopped a suitable time later to check out the situation. If quizzed he could claim not to have seen the accident and deny any knowledge of the truck. He would know she was alive and that might have led to the phone message. Probably she was still being watched so they would know I was here. If we continued with the questioning it could lead to further trouble. We needed to be careful.

"I don't understand what this is all about, but I think you are still in danger. We should go to the police."

"Peter, the police were not interested when I told them I had been run off the road. I was just a silly emotional old woman! Do you think I will get any better understanding if I go to a station and say someone is trying to kill me!"

Suzie was right. There was no proof of a truck forcing her off the road. A young man driving too fast had had a car crash forty-one years ago and a girl had disappeared around the same time. Police had already investigated that crash and the disappearance and found nothing. All we had was a three word message on a phone answering machine.

Still someone wanted to kill her. I decided it might be best if Suzie and I vanished for a time.

"We seem to be intruding where we are not wanted. I think it would be best if we very obviously distance ourselves from here. Let them think we have given up on whatever they are worried about."

"I am not running away from anything!"

"I understand your feelings, I don't want to either but it may be the best way to get them off our back, whoever they are. If they think we are frightened they may relax and lose interest in us. We can still try to find out what is behind all this but we do need to be very, very discreet."

"What do you suggest?"

"How about a holiday for few days? I know a great place

far away. Two rooms, I promise."

"No, one room, please."

Suzie may have suggested one room while we were away, but here in her home I had the guest bedroom. I wasn't the first man to use it. I think it had been frequently used by another man. A very small man from the look of the books on the bedside table and the blue lion and grey koala sitting on the pillow. I could imagine Suzie lying on the bed, perhaps even snuggled up in the bed, reading stories to her grandson. I wondered what would have happened if we had stayed together. What would our kids have been like? Would they have been like hers? Although they now both lived in Australia I gathered they still had strong English accents from their childhood. Perhaps they would have been more like my son. Suzie seemed very close to her children although I gathered she did not always approve of her daughter's decisions. Emma sounded a very strong willed and independent woman. I wondered whether she might be too much like her mother for them not to clash on occasions.

I drifted off to sleep, watched over by a blue lion and a grey koala, wondering who else might be watching us.

16 ESCAPE TO HAYMAN

Suzie

Just as the cabin crew were about to close the aircraft's door a tall heavily tattooed man entered the plane. As he walked past he looked very closely at me. He was wearing a black singlet with a raised fist on it. He was deeply tanned with close cropped hair. One tattoo I noticed was of a Eureka flag and another was of two crossed pistols. He wore blue sunnies that hid his eyes. The effect was threatening. I didn't like the look he gave me. I leant in closer to Peter, and whispered my concern. Peter turned and looked. The blue sunnies were still on me. It appeared our escape charade had not worked.

All during the flight to Sydney I was conscious of the blue sunglasses five rows behind us.

We changed planes at Sydney. When we took our seats on the flight for Hamilton Island he was five rows behind us again, still looking at me. I leant even closer to Peter.

As the plane took off I felt Peter's hand touch me and he pointed out the window. Below us was Sydney Harbour in all its glory. We seemed to be so close to the high rise offices of the CBD, and to the Bridge and the Opera House: the icons of the city. It was a beautiful clear blue day. The water sparkled and I could see the white tracks of the boats moving on the harbour. There was a big cruise ship docked at the passenger terminal, ferries rushing back and forward to Circular Quay, and a mass of smaller boats. Yachts with their billowing sails, motor cruisers, and smaller runabouts and fishing boats seemed to fill the Harbour. Scattered around every inlet and bay were even more boats, berthed in marinas or tied to buoys or at anchor.

I had flown into Sydney a number of times, usually from the south, and I had only once flown over the harbour. That day had been grey and cold and the harbour had lacked the life and colour that was now below us. Peter explained, that in order to minimise noise for locals, flights usually took off over Botany Bay and the ocean. Today the strong winds from the north east meant that we had used runway 34, and then turned east after take-off. Our track took us out towards the ocean, before turning north to pick up our flight path to the Whitsundays.

Below us the harbour gave way to housing and then timbered country which I assumed was a national park. Through the aeroplane's windows I could see fingers of water tracking up the floors of valleys. Smaller clusters of boats were moored in some of the inlets but nothing like the number on Sydney Harbour. I realised we must be near Broken Bay and Pitt Water. I remembered that Peter had told me he lived on the edge of Sydney near Pitt Water. I wondered where his house was and what it would be like. Would it be an old house, or a modern house? I couldn't see him in a modern glass box although I imagine the views could be very beautiful overlooking the waters. He had said his wife loved native plants so perhaps it would be a timber bungalow blending into the bush. Who would have made the decision on buying or building the house? Peter or his wife? They had lived there for many years so perhaps it was built in a style fashionable in the late seventies or early eighties. I touched Peter's arm and asked where he lived. He looked out the window and pointed behind us.

Then I found myself wondering what Peter's life was like. How had he adapted to the loss of his wife? He was obviously very fond of her. Was he a lonely widower? What would he be like in the kitchen, could he cook? I imagined there would be plenty of women who would consider him a good catch. He was an engineer so I imagined the house would be neat and tidy. Everything would work, unlike the houses of some of my more creative friends. One in particular always caused me concern when I visited her home. The untidy clutter of her books and paintings was bad enough but it was her lack of interest in cleaning the dirt and grime that really irritated me. I was sure she saw me as anal retentive in my housekeeping. My thoughts returned to Peter. Had he had women in his life since his wife's death? Would I be the first?

My mind went back to Blue Sunnies sitting five rows behind us. When I had returned from the aircraft toilet he was still there looking at me. He would hardly attack us in mid-air. That would be unlikely. What would he do when we landed? Was he just watching us or did he have orders to silence us somehow? It couldn't be a car crash. There were no roads where we were going. Perhaps a boating accident! Drowning in the swimming pool! Poison in the food! I told myself I really was becoming paranoid. Anyway Peter would be there to help me. Perhaps Blue Sunnies meant to do us both in!

I was puzzled. I knew we were going to Hayman Island and that meant we had to fly north to Hamilton Island before transferring to Hayman by boat. I had assumed that our flight would be over ocean but we seemed to spend hours over land, yet Sydney was on the coast and the island would be off the coast. It was only when I looked at the airline magazine I realized that with the bulge of Australia to the east we would have to pass Rockhampton before we would be approaching the coastline again.

The sea when it reappeared was the blue of all the tourist brochures. Scattered over the sea were tiny islands. Our plane descended and circled the single runway built onto the side of one of the larger islands. We had arrived at Hamilton Island. Walking down the steps from the plane I suddenly became aware of the warmth. In Melbourne the season was changing to autumn. It was still warm but some days there was a chill in the mornings and in the evenings. Here the feel was different, the sea breeze gentle and the air warm. The travel agents often spoke of balmy weather. This was what they meant.

Peter

After our plane had taken off it commenced a turn to the east. I touched Suzie on the arm and pointed out the view of the Harbour. A few minutes later we turned again and I could just pick out my house amongst the bush of Pitt Water as we tracked north. By the time Suzie asked where I lived we had already passed it and I could only point behind us. Claire and I had lived there for many years. It held so many memories. Now I was flying off to a romantic island resort with another woman. Claire was no longer here but in some way it still felt disrespectful. What would it be like to have another woman in our home? I knew it happened all the time—but for other people. Death, divorce and sometimes just deceit. People's lives moved on, but it would still be a very emotional moment for me if Suzie ever visited the house in the bush.

Suzie was very quiet on our flight to Hamilton Island. She appeared to be lost in thought. Was she having second thoughts about coming away with me, especially since she had stipulated one bed? Or was it something else? The tattooed man with the blue sunglasses was obviously disturbing her. Was he really some thug watching our movements? The thought I had put out of my mind when we had first discussed the attempt to run her off the road returned. Was she really being honest with me? Or was there something in her past she was not telling me? The man with blue sunglasses had the look of someone who could be physically intimidating. He was young and muscular. I was well past my prime. If he threatened any violence I was unlikely to be his match. I hoped Suzie would make a good tag team. That would be our only chance if things got rough.

I had been to Hayman Island years ago with Claire. We had celebrated a success that I had had on the share market with a promising copper explorer I had been watching. We had loved the resort. The Whitsundays had been beautiful then, and today the shades of blue in the sea and sky and the white of the clouds and the beaches were just as lovely. In my years of travel with mining work I had managed to see many renowned beauty spots, but for me the Whitsundays rate right at the top. The resort, the only one on the island, had always been a great place to escape from the world. The gardens were beautiful, the island perfect for daydreaming of beachcombing, of white beaches and of beautiful sunsets over the sea. There the dream became the reality. As well, the restaurants and bars were superb. Unlike Hamilton Island where our plane had landed, Hayman was small, uncrowded and exclusive. Day trippers were not welcome and most people arrived on the resort's launches or by helicopter or sea plane.

Suzie

As we waited for our luggage to be unloaded Blue Sunnies was still watching me. Then suddenly he had his arms around a young woman and two pretty blonde girls.

He walked over to me.

"I must apologise for looking at you so much. You remind me of my mother. You look so alike, she died last year. It was almost as if I was seeing her again."

A feeling of relief flooded over me. Blue Sunnies was not the hit man of my fears. He was a chef on Hamilton Island returning to his family after visiting Melbourne for his brother's fortieth birthday.

When we walked out of the terminal at the end of the island runway, the Hayman launch was waiting at the adjoining wharf for the trip through the Whitsundays to the Island itself.

Peter

The gleaming white boat was at the wharf across from the airport terminal. A crewman dressed all in white took our luggage and another welcomed us aboard and noted our names. A hostess proffered a glass of champagne or an alternate drink and then a plate of tiny sandwiches and other nibbles. When the passenger list was complete the boat pulled away from the wharf. Soon we were away from the harbour and the captain opened up the twin engines. Sitting on the top sundeck watching the islands appear and disappear, a glass of better than usual champagne in our hands, on a boat that seemed to be out of the lives of the rich and famous, was a pleasure. I wondered what Suzie was thinking. She certainly had the look and the poise that fitted the lifestyle. Even in a pair of jeans and a t-shirt she could look a million dollars. What had her life been like? She had only told me a little of the years since I had known her in London. I had discovered she had worked in public relations but she had given no other details. From her house and car she must have had a good income—or a good divorce settlement. So much was still left unsaid and a mystery. I remembered her as being open about her life when I had first met her. Even now she seemed the same but how well did I really know her?

"This is so beautiful. I have seen photos of the Whitsundays but I have never been here. I used to go to the Greek Islands, years ago, and I loved them but this is even more beautiful."

I was pleased Suzie found the Whitsundays as beautiful as I did. Fifty minutes later we pulled into the resort jetty. A buggy was waiting to take us straight to our room. All the formalities had been completed on the boat. The luggage followed.

17 SUNSHINE AND SEX

Suzie

The bed was huge. White and virginal. It was the first thing I saw when we walked into the room. I couldn't take my eyes away from it. I had suggested one bed and this was it. On an island resort it surely couldn't be as virginal as it looked.

It was a long time since I had been a virgin. Boyfriends, husband, two children and a divorce had all happened since that time. Although I had lived in London following the freedom of the sixties, I had never really joined in the easy going way that some people treated sex. Not that I was a virgin when I first met Peter, but I guess with my country upbringing and church school education I was by nature reserved when it came to sex.

Even after my divorce I hadn't jumped wildly into the world of sex as several of my friends had done.

There had been opportunities and I had taken some of them. Romantic weekends at pretty B&Bs in the hills, trips away, stage shows and dinners with the usual arrangements. Some had been fun and I had no regrets, but none had ever developed into anything.

When I thought about it I could hardly claim to have had lots of partners. There had been the occasional one night stand but I had never felt comfortable afterwards. I had certainly never had a partner. When I thought of partner it sounded like a long term serious relationship and that had never happened for me. Well perhaps almost with one man, but that had ended.

These days the young talk of 'friends with benefits'. That had never worked for me either. I didn't want to lose good friends by complicating our friendship and the 'benefits' had never turned into friendship. Thinking about it I guess I had just given up on sex as too much trouble and not worth the hassle. Not that I didn't enjoy a good tumble. My ex had certainly been that and I had enjoyed our times until I found out that he was sharing himself around.

And I had enjoyed making love with Peter all those years ago. What was it about him? Even then I was the one who had made the play. Looking back I had decided almost from the time I first saw him that I wanted to sleep with him. Peter had certainly not been unreceptive to my advances. Yet normally I was the cool standoffish girl that knocked back such invitations and never the one to make the suggestion.

Even here it was me who said one room when he had suggested this trip. He had given me the opportunity for two rooms, and looked quizzically at me when making the booking and found the room had a double bed. What was I thinking! I couldn't take my eyes off the bed.

"What a view."

I looked at Peter. I'm here, and all I'm thinking of is beds and sex and all he sees is the sea!

He was standing on the balcony looking out to the sea. It was many shades of the beautiful blues for which the Whitsundays are famous. Below our room was a huge lagoon pool and just beyond were the white sands of the beach. Garden walkways fringed with palms and ferns and colourful tropical plants led off between the buildings.

What will it be like to sleep with Peter again? The last time, two days before I ran away to Germany had been special. I think that was what made me leave. I knew if it happened again I would want to stay with him forever. Yet it wasn't just the sex, good though it was. I have had better from other men. It was just with him it was somehow special. What would it be like now? I had said one room! I knew what would happen if I shared a bed with him. I wondered if he felt the same way. He must know what will happen. He knew in London. What will he think of me? I'm not the same girl I was forty years ago. Then everything was firm and almost unblemished. Today I have loose skin, my boobs are floppy—well not too bad really. I was never big in that department so gravity has not taken too much of a hold. Its ages since I've been to the hairdresser, and I'm sure my hair is showing where it needs a touch up to cover the grey. Blotches are showing on my skin. Thinking back we were both fairly athletic then but these days, I don't think, well I know, I am not as flexible as I used to be.

Besides, what will he be like? He seems healthy and fit enough, although he doesn't have the look of a gym junkie or that lean tanned look of bike riders. Actually what do I really know about him? We have talked about lots of things but there is still so much I don't know. Can he perform? He's not young anymore. Well, nor am I. Will he want sex? I hope so! How will I feel if he doesn't want me?

"How about we change and go down to the pool? It would be nice lying there soaking up the sun and the sound of the waves. I will buy you a drink if you wish. I'll stay out here while you change."

That's Peter, I thought, always the gentleman and considerate. I wasn't ready to be seen naked in daylight, even my one piece bathing costume showed more than I would have preferred, and it was years old and out of fashion. There had been no time to buy a new one in our rush to get away.

Peter

As I remembered from my stay with Claire the rooms were large and very comfortable. Glass doors opened onto a balcony overlooking the pool and sea. Even with the two chairs and a table there was still lots of space on the balcony. The room itself had another table and chairs, several armchairs and a coffee table. The usual large television was on a table against the wall. Behind the bed shutters opened into the dressing room and beyond the dressing room lay the marble bathroom with a huge shower recess and large bath. All in all I felt pleased with the effect. On our visit to Hayman, Claire and I had enjoyed the luxury and environment of the resort. I felt a stab of pain thinking of Claire. Should I have brought another women to this place? Should I have picked a different island? It was four years now since she had died. We had always said that if anything happened to either of us then the survivor should get on with their life. Even when she knew she had only a year to live she had said the same thing. Still it was strange to be here with a woman who was not Claire. Even stranger to be with a woman from my past who had disappeared from my life so many years ago. It was not like me to proposition a woman to come away with me on a holiday. Yet it had seemed like the best solution to escape from the troubles in Melbourne. I was surprised when she had said yes, even more when she had suggested one room. I had surprised myself when I had asked her. It was not like me. Ever since I had married Claire there had never been another woman in my life. Sure I knew some very attractive women but Claire was all I had wanted.

What would life have been like if Suzie had not disappeared? Obviously there had been a connection, a bond, between us. From the first day we had met we just wanted to be with each other. It was fun to be together and we had quickly gravitated to sleeping together. Then she had disappeared. Even now I didn't know why. When I tried to find out from her friends where she was they wouldn't tell me. I was sure she had told them not to say where she had gone. She had still not explained her disappearance apart from saying that she had to go to Germany. I had even wondered if she might have gotten pregnant. There was hardly time for her to know, and it wasn't likely. She had always seemed so confident and in control. I couldn't see her having an abortion or giving a child away for adoption. That just would not have been the woman I knew—or thought I knew. Besides, her son was similar in age to my son Matthew, so she was probably not pregnant at that time.

It was several years after Suzie when I first met Claire. I did worry for a while that I was on the rebound and not really over Suzie. Claire and Suzie were quite different in many ways but they both had the same spirit for life and a generosity of nature that I found attractive. Claire had made a great mate for a wandering miner. I don't know that Suzie would have adjusted to that life as well as Claire had done. It certainly wasn't what Suzie had seen for herself. I don't know how we would have fared if she had not disappeared. Perhaps it would have ended badly. How strange that now we should be back in each other's company.

Sleeping together had always been a pleasure. I remembered the feeling of waking beside her. And our time awake had been fun. The sex had been open and happy and energetic. There had been lots of laughter. What would it be like now? She must realise that one room meant one bed and one bed meant things would happen. Well I hope things will happen. It has been a while since I last performed in bed. Could I still do it? She was very attractive. That shouldn't be a problem but would she be satisfied? I am sure there would have been men looking to romance her and bed her. I'm sure that she would have had offers. I really don't fit the type for handsome. I am probably carrying a bit too much weight and my hair is thinning, well more than thinning, actually missing on my forehead and crown if I am honest. Nor am I the most groomed and polished of men. Even my best friends tell me I need to rely on personality, not looks. They also suggested money would be even more helpful. I am comfortable, hardly rich, but enough for a good life. Would it be enough for Suzie? Now I am even thinking of a life together with her! That is a bit premature. Premature! Oh I hope that is not the case. I'm sure when we are in bed things will happen but I don't want that to happen.

"How about we change and go down to the pool. It would be nice lying there soaking up the sun and the sound of the waves. I will buy you a drink if you wish. I'll stay out here while you change. Later we can make a booking for one of the restaurants for dinner. I have been told the Asian restaurant is recommended."

Suzie approved of my suggestion.

Suzie

Dinner in the Bamboo Restaurant was a delight. The food was a mix of many Asian influences. Some Thai, some Chinese and even a bit of Indian. It was the setting that added to the charm. As the name suggested the tables were in the open, in a grove of bamboos and tropical plants. The night was balmy and such a change from the cooler nights of Melbourne. The light was soft and it was a night for romance. The courses were small but flavoursome and we swapped tastes with each other. Peter's choice of Riesling was perfect with the food. But still I could not escape from one thought.

"Peter. What do you think will happen when we get back to Melbourne?"

As wonderful as the evening was the thought in the back of my mind was why we were here. We were running away. But from whom and why? What was waiting for us on our return? I was sure Peter would have the same feeling.

"I think we should lie low. Pretend that nothing had happened. That it was just an accident. I think we should be very careful not to attract any attention."

"You said pretend. What about the phone call? We can't say that didn't happen. You obviously believe it wasn't an accident that I was run off the road. You think that something is going on. Are you going to let it pass or do we do something about it? If you want to go back to Sydney that's fine but I want to know what it is all about."

"So do I, Suzie, but I think we should be very careful. Whoever is behind it is dangerous. They didn't care if you were killed. That's why we need to be cautious. I think we must let them think we have moved on. Let's take a bottle of bubbly back to the room and celebrate."

"What are we celebrating?"

"How about that we are here, it's a beautiful night and we are together."

"I saw a half bottle of bubbly in the fridge in the room. That will be enough. I want you relaxed but not too relaxed."

"You're a wicked woman, Suzie Benedict."

"Just wait and see how wicked I am."

The bubbles and chocolate were delicious. I'm not sure if they made Peter relax but they certainly did me. My bluster about being wicked had seemed like fun when I made it but now the moment was almost here. I went into the bathroom and changed into my nightie. This time I had packed my best, the sexiest one I owned, rather the red flannelette pyjamas that I wore for Melbourne winters. My silk nightie had not had much use. Should I remove my make up or not? It was years since I had worried about that question. It comes off, well except for a little around the eyes and I had better use some more perfume. When I emerged from the bathroom Peter was in bed. Clothes on, or off? I decided to leave my nightie on. I slipped into the bed beside him. He was wearing boxer shorts. I reached over to touch him and felt hair. Not just some hair on his head but on his chest! And his shoulders! And on his back! I don't like the look of hairy men and here I am in bed with one. He wasn't hairy when I knew him in London, but that was so long ago. He has changed. Then I felt his hand reach out.

When I woke the sun was shining through the open doors of the balcony. We had left the doors open to listen to the sound of the surf rolling in, and to feel the gentle breeze off the sea. That night, lying in bed we had looked out and seen the mass of stars in the heavens. Living in the city I had forgotten how many there were and how bright they could be.

I lay still. I could hear Peter's soft breathing.

When he stirred I moved.

"Good morning darling." He reached out and laid his arm across the pillows. Without thinking I moved closer and laid my head in the crook of his arm. As our bodies touched I realised we were still naked. Somehow this morning I was no longer concerned by his hairy body. I just felt comfortable and secure lying with him.

"What would you like to do today, wicked woman?"

"I would like to take a walk around the gardens. They look lovely and the tropical plants are so different to the ones I know in Melbourne. Then perhaps we could try the other pool."

"Can I have breakfast first?"

"Of course, but first."

The resort grounds were worth the time taken to explore

them. The hotel had spent a huge amount of time and money in developing them as a feature of the resort. They obviously had a passionate team maintaining them.

The plants were so different from those I was familiar with in Melbourne. The island, although tropical, was in a rain shadow and the hills were covered in scraggly native trees and bushes reflecting the dryer winter season. However the grounds of the resort had been transformed. Palm trees were scattered through the gardens, the golf course, the tennis courts and walkways. The walkways were lined with beds profuse with varieties of ferns, flaxes, cycads, cannas and bromeliads. Jasmine scented the air and the cool ponds were fringed with crotons and heliconias and gingers. Orchids hung from trees and colourful bougainvilleas hung from planters on balconies. The largest ponds were covered with waterlilies across which dusky moorhens walked while two swans sailed elegantly in another lily edged lagoon. My favourite was a rock-wall of tillandsia with its multi-hued flowers.

On our walk we had seen the resort shop with the usual clothing, swim suits, hats and towels.

Peter had suggested I might need a new swim suit. He had seen a bikini that would suit me. It was gorgeous, but not for me. Perhaps years ago I would have loved it but now I needed something a little less revealing. There were stretchmarks and a scar from Emma's birth that needed hiding. In a soft light they weren't too bad but they certainly didn't need public exposure in full daylight. I did agree to a lovely two piece that hid the problems and was still very flattering.

"Your female vanity is showing."

"What do you mean?"

"I've been watching you look at yourself in the mirror. You look great."

I admitted to myself I did like to look good, and I had seen young women in briefer bikinis that didn't look as good as I could, but I certainly was not going to admit that to Peter.

Peter paid for the swimsuit. It was a strange feeling. It was so long since a man had bought me clothing. Even Tony had rarely bought me clothes, although he was always generous with cash or paid my credit card when I did buy something.

"Now it's my turn. I want a shirt for you. I am not going to the pool if you are wearing that hideous yellow number with frangipanis and hibiscus on it. Where did you get it?"

"I bought it in Noosa. A few of us went there for a week's holiday several years ago. I thought I needed something holidayish."

"Did your wife buy your clothes?"

"No."

"So that was your own choice?"

"Yes. I needed something for the beach."

"This would look much better."

I had picked out a stylish shirt in a soft white cotton voile. Casual and not too smart or trendy. I did want Peter to wear it!

Again his card came out.

"No, this one is on me. I don't want to be a bought woman! Now the flower garden goes to the rubbish bin. Maybe someone with retro taste in bad Hawaiian detective shows will like it."

Lying around the pool was bliss. I even forgot why we were there. We talked and caught up on all the events that had happened in our lives. We talked of kids and my grandchild. We talked of old friends and of each other's friends since the London days. I spoke of my life after I had first met Peter and left for Germany. Eventually even the shade lounges weren't enough and we had had sufficient sun. We decided to go back to the room for a coffee.

While the jug was boiling Peter scanned through some magazines lying on the table. One was a business magazine. Suddenly he stopped. I passed him his coffee and he showed me the article. It was about a successful businessman. It was a rags to riches story. Poor boy from rural Victoria makes good as head of major real estate, construction and development company.

He had started out helping the local greengrocer with packing shelves and deliveries to earn extra money to help support his parents and siblings. When he left school he moved to Ballarat and got a job with a building company. While he lacked trade qualifications he quickly picked up the business side. He and some partners then went into a hotel investment. It didn't work, and putting his future on the line, he bought out his partners in a vendor deal and turned it around. From that springboard he moved to Melbourne and developed suburban housing blocks for the growing city. Always heavily in debt he had branched out into building houses and then into ready-mix cement, building supplies and landscaping.

Like many such entrepreneurs he had had his ups and downs but had survived. During a boom in the property market he merged most of his businesses into a new company and listed it on the stock market, raising additional funding and freeing up cash to expand. This new company was Sovereign Corporation—real estate, construction, building materials, hotels and its latest project, a joint public/private partnership with the government to develop a large parcel of land in the CBD.

Now the poor boy from the bush was a major businessman with interests throughout Australia and Asia. He was well known as a major benefactor of charities in Melbourne and a man with connections.

It was the usual sort of piece that appears from time to time in the financial press, sometimes with assistance from the company PR section. There was a photo of him standing beside a two tone green Rolls Royce outside his home. What caught Peter's eye was a photo of his original office. The name 'Grande Developments' was in the same font as the 'Grande Imperial'.

The man was Bernard Mayne.

Was it possible that Bernard Mayne was our Bernie James who had moved on from SP bookmaking and invitation-only gambling sessions at his hotel to greater business success?

Our questions about Ballarat and the hotel might, just might, have attracted his attention. Illegal gambling might explain his rapid financial climb but would hardly warrant death threats.

Yet what other link could there be? Our trouble began when we asked questions about Ballarat. Billy had died in a car crash near Ballarat. Nobody knew why he was going there, if that was where he was going. With him there had never been any suggestion of foul play, unlike my accident.

Merry and I had visited Ballarat for a girl's weekend celebration when I had started my teaching career. As far as anyone knew Merry hadn't been back to Ballarat since that weekend.

There didn't seem to be any connections. Certainly not enough to try to kill me.

And yet 'ask no questions' had to be linked to something in Ballarat.

There was one more photo. It showed Mayne in front of 'Elysium Gardens', his newest real estate development on the edge of Melbourne. In the background was a large white tip truck!

"I think we should look into that when we go back to Melbourne, but it may be best if we have a few more days here. Rushing back would look strange. It may attract their attention again. For now let's just enjoy the coffee and the view."

Peter's plan seemed very sensible and attractive.

"Are you still enjoying looking out at the sea?"

"No. I meant the view inside. You!"

Peter can seem so serious at times but then he softens. He already knows how to press my buttons.

What more can a girl want?

18 RETURN TO UNCERTAINTY

Suzie

The flights back to Melbourne were much less stressful than our flights to Hayman had been. At least this time I didn't have the thought of some tattooed thug watching my every movement. The Hayman launch returned us to the Hamilton Island airport where we had to fill in an hour and a half due to a flight delay. That gave Peter and me time to walk down to the boat harbour, grab a snack, and admire the beautiful yachts tied to the wharves. It was much more pleasant than sitting around an airport lounge and eating the usual airport fare. This time our flight didn't approach Sydney over the Harbour, but flew down along the coastline, past the Heads, and gave us a wonderful view looking up the Harbour to the Bridge. Unfortunately the delay also meant a full aeroplane out of Sydney as the first of the afternoon rush of returning business day-trippers caught flights for their homes in Melbourne.

We had left Hayman with a cloudless blue sky and warm weather. As we approached Melbourne the weather turned grey and it started to drizzle. I noticed Peter's mood changing with the weather. Perhaps it wasn't the weather but the fact that we were coming back to uncertainty because I also felt my mood become more and more sombre the closer we came to my home in Melbourne. I think Peter was sharing my fears. What were we going to do?

"Will they be waiting for us?"

Like Peter I had decided there must be more than one. If it was Mayne I couldn't see him driving a truck and trying to run me off the road himself. Nor could I see him standing on a street corner watching my house, or worse, Max and Amelia's house. He was too important and wealthy to do that. Peter's reply that they would be unlikely to have someone waiting at the airport on the off chance we might return was reassuring until he added that he doubted that whoever it was would have lost interest in me completely. Hopefully they would have watched us leave but they would probably be keeping an eye on my house in case I returned.

"What do you think we should do?"

Peter suggested we needed to find out more about Bernard Mayne.

In the taxi from the airport I phoned my son and daughter to tell them of my return. I had told them I was going away for a break with a friend. While they knew of my accident I hadn't given them all the details, nor had I mentioned the friend I was going away with was a man, and certainly not someone I knew before I met their father. They hadn't needed to know that just yet.

The house was as we had left it. I dropped my luggage in my bedroom and Peter went towards the guest bedroom. I took his hand and led him, with his suitcase, into my bedroom.

"We have been sleeping together for days. You don't have to move to another room just because you are back in my home. It is too late for that. If I sleep with you somewhere then I will sleep with you here."

Peter smiled.

After I had poured drinks we sat in the lounge room and tried to come up with a plan of action. Too many questions would only attract attention and that could prove fatal if it was Mayne behind the attack. Therefore it would be unwise to go around publically seeking information from some of my friends who might know of him. Peter was insistent that we remain very discreet. But if we were discreet how would we find out what we needed to know? I suggested Ian Holmes. With his contacts he was sure to know something about Mayne, or at least put us in contact with the right person. Peter was cautious about approaching Ian. The trouble had started after I had spoken to Ian and Roley.

Our ideas were going in circles without coming up with a workable plan when Emma arrived. She gave me a hug and said she was worried about a car parked in the street with a man sitting in it. She was concerned that someone may be watching the neighbourhood and planning a possible break in. Even before any introductions Peter and I both rushed to the window to look for the car.

"What are you doing?" Our strange behaviour had startled Emma.

The car began to move off slowly. Further down the street, lights came on in a garden, a gate opened and the car drove into the driveway with the gate closing behind it. Someone had found the address they were searching for, or perhaps had phoned ahead to have the gate opened.

Emma was puzzled by our rush to the window and the way we had furtively looked out. It was certainly not my usual behaviour. How was I to explain our behaviour? First I had to introduce Peter.

My daughter had often told me I should have a man in my life, usually when she was in one of her own relationships. When that relationship soured the story would change to women must have their independence. Now that it appeared that I may have someone she seemed very ambivalent about the idea. Although I thought it was rather premature to consider Peter a relationship, even if I had slept with him for four nights—which Emma didn't know about anyway.

Over dinner she quizzed Peter about his life. I thought of my father subtly sounding out my ex-husband and remembered how I had ignored his gentle suggestion that I should think carefully before committing. I was young, I was in love, and as much as I loved my father I would have ignored any criticism of Tony. It was only years later I realised how accurately my father had summed up the situation.

Peter was very careful in avoiding any mention of the car crash or our relationship, saying only that we had been good friends many years ago and he had suggested that a break after the crash might be good medicine.

I could sense Emma was finding Peter very conservative in his views. He was so different to her usual companions. Peter was going to be a problem for her, and that would be a problem for me.

Finally I decided that I must tell her the truth about the crash, and how I had been driven off the road. I also told her about Peter and our trips to Oakleigh and Ballarat looking into the disappearance of Merry. She had heard the story of Merry, but it was long ago, before she had been born, and the story had never been important to her.

"Mum, you have to go to the police!"

I told her of my experience on the night of the crash and Peter explained that really we had nothing definite to work with. The police would see her mother as a silly lady with some cock and bull story.

Emma turned angrily to Peter.

"Why have you got my mother into this?"

Peter's attempt to explain that it had nothing to do with him was not accepted by Emma. No amount of explanation improved his position. Even my attempt to support his explanations was not accepted.

While Peter and I were clearing away the meal and washing up plates, Emma, who had gone off to the bathroom, reappeared. Walking past the bedroom she had seen Peter's suitcase open in my bedroom. She beckoned me into the hallway.

"Mum, are you sleeping with that man?"

From the tone of her voice she didn't approve. Whether it was Peter, or any man, I wasn't sure, but I suspected that Peter was definitely even less acceptable than any other man. This time I put my foot down. I had nursed her through many of her emotional dramas. I was not going to have my daughter decide my life for me.

"Yes, he is a good man. I like being with him and I intend to spend more time with him. You should give him a chance and not take an instant dislike to him."

Emma went very quiet. She was polite to Peter but soon found a reason to excuse herself.

Peter

Suzie was unsettled after Emma left. We returned to trying to develop a plan of action with regards to Mayne, however it was clear her mind was no longer on the problem.

The phone rang and Suzie answered it. She left me in the lounge room and walked into the kitchen with the phone. While I couldn't hear the conversation, from her manner and the few words that drifted through the open doorway, it was someone she knew.

She came back into the room and replaced the phone.

"It was my son, Max. Emma has already phoned him. He was upset I hadn't told him that the crash wasn't an accident. He is concerned about what may happen. Emma has also been on to him about the man in my life. It appears that is what you now are. She doesn't approve of you. At least Max didn't appear so concerned though I suspect you will have another inspection tomorrow night."

"What did I do to upset your daughter?"

"Emma has very fixed ideas. She is very much an inner city person. Always concerned with some issue, or saving something or someone. I suspect in you she sees all the evils of the world. She sees you as a conservative, right wing male chauvinist who wants to dig up the world and pollute what is left. Worse you have been sleeping with her mother. She can't understand how I can find you attractive."

"Would you be happier if I left, or at least moved into the bedroom with the blue lion?"

"No. Whether you agree or not, I guess you are now officially the man in my life. The kids will just have to accept their mother's wishes. I don't know that it will be all that much fun tonight, but you are still very welcome in my bed. We will just have to see what tomorrow brings."

19 WEB SEARCH

Peter

I woke to find Suzie gone. Her side of the bed was cold but I could hear noises coming from the kitchen. As I lay half-awake I wondered what sort of breakfast she would have in her own home. Would it be light and healthy, or something more substantial that I would enjoy? Breakfast when you are on holidays is often quite a different affair. The Hayman breakfasts with optional champagne and fruit juice and a huge selection of delights were a treat that I had indulged in—perhaps even overindulged. Omelettes were always my favourite when I was away from home and staying in a big hotel. My omelettes at home never seemed to taste as good.

I wondered what her son would be like. She had been very certain that we would receive a visit from him when he finished work. I definitely hadn't impressed her daughter. That brought me to thinking of my son. What will Matthew think when I tell him about Suzie? He was probably a little younger than Emma, more likely the same age as Suzie's son. I always found it hard to put ages on people. With his work on the North West Shelf gas fields it was unlikely that he would meet Suzie for some time. Perhaps we could do a video call. While we were close I didn't know how he would respond to a woman in my life. Would he think it a good idea, or would he see it as a desertion of his mother? I recalled I was now considered 'the man in Suzie's life'. It seemed to have happened without either of us making any decisions. It had just happened. It was not an unpleasant thought but I wasn't sure just what it meant. I didn't think either of us had given it any consideration. What now? Where do we go from here?

More importantly, what are we going to do about Mayne? How do we find out more about him? Where should we start looking? What are we looking for? What do we really need to find?

We know Mayne was involved in Ballarat. The article in the magazine had said he had an interest in a hotel there before he came to Melbourne, however the article had never stated which hotel. The only link was the font used for Mayne's business 'Grande Developments'. It was the same font as the 'Grande Imperial'. That would hardly be a coincidence. The suspect gambling rooms had been at the Grande, although the hotel licensee was found to be innocent. But was Mayne involved with the hotel at the time of the gambling raid? The photo of the proprietor of the Grande was very indistinct. It could have been almost anyone and the newspaper had not mentioned any names.

I decided nothing was being solved by lying in bed. I had better rise. I found Suzie in the kitchen making some sort of juice concoction. She had had a restless night. Her daughter's comments were still troubling her. After breakfast we started work.

It was obvious we needed to find some solid facts and

where better to start than the Internet. Perhaps we would find something about Mayne that either linked him to our troubles, or completely removed him from any further consideration. He was easy to find. Page after page of links appeared. Newspaper stories, PR guff, magazine stories, society notes, sports pages. He was everywhere.

The man was a well-known identity in Melbourne but had interests all around the country as well as overseas.

A good church man with big gifts to the Catholic Church for good works. Photos with the Archbishop. Mayne at the football. Photos with the team he sponsored. Donations to political parties. Photos with the leaders of both parties: it seemed to depend on who was in power, or about to come to power. Mayne always seemed to time his donations to causes and parties to perfection. The man also had a taste for culture. A supporter of opera. A significant donor to the Art Gallery. The same art gallery where this had all begun with a cup of coffee and a face and body that seemed familiar. Little had I realised where she would lead me. I wondered whether this was always the case with her, and what else she would lead me into.

His business interests were wide. Various websites told the story of the young man made good. He was a country boy who had managed to buy a parcel of land on the outskirts of Melbourne just as the city was expanding. One small subdivision led to another and each subdivision was larger. Then he had moved onto building houses on his subdivisions and from there into a real estate business. Timber yards, whitegoods, gravel pits and ready-mix cement were added, and then a trucking company. One website showed photos of a fleet of ready-mix concrete trucks, white tip trucks unloading gravel or landscaping materials, and semitrailers loaded with steel framing and roofing material. Each business had expanded beyond its original purpose of supplying only his own development needs.

It was one of these developments, the 'Elysium Gardens', on the outskirts of Melbourne that we had seen on our train trip to Ballarat.

He had floated several of his interests on the stock exchange and they were well covered by the financial press. From housing he had expanded these companies into high rise apartments and office blocks. Like many developers he had faced financial difficulties during downturns in the economy but had always managed to survive. He seemed to be able to pick up sufficient government tenants to struggle through until the next upturn. Like most large companies the annual reports contained a list of subsidiaries, some wholly owned, some partly owned. They were the usual sort. Companies acquired in takeovers, companies registered in different jurisdictions, companies for tax purposes and nominee companies, Nominee No. 1, No. 2, No. 25 etcetera.

At present he was tendering for his biggest project ever. A public/private partnership to redevelop a whole city block. This was based on government and private tenants for three office towers, private apartments, a shopping mall and an international hotel. It would be the jewel in his crown. Finance was in place with a group of bankers, the government was guaranteeing occupancy of several towers, and all was ready to start work subject to a final government probity check on the company and Mayne personally.

Nowhere was there a mention of the Grande Imperial hotel at Ballarat, although the new hotel was to carry the name of the company and be called the Sovereign Grande.

There was no indication of what Mayne had done to get some cash together before his arrival in Melbourne.

Somehow the nagging thought remained that perhaps not all his businesses were listed on the web. A man like him would have private family companies as well. With his operations in the construction industry he would be sure to have had dealings with people who had mates with tattoos and heavy handed ways of resolving disputes. Also some of the articles we found in the financial press had hinted, very tentatively, that some of the deals had unexplained features which could cause the reader to suspect corruption. Land had been rezoned, building restrictions changed, objections overruled. Not that the press dared to suggest wrongdoing. Mayne was known to employ aggressive and expensive legal counsel.

Nothing on the web came close to any link with our troubles. Certainly he was a successful businessman who probably cut corners when it suited, and burnished his image with good works while he oiled away any troubles with the profits from his deals. Unlike some in similar positions he didn't appear to cream off the best profits to his private accounts while leaving only slim pickings and higher risk for the general investors in his listed companies.

Then I saw it!

On the fifth page of the search listings.

"Grande Ideas—Heads I win, tails you lose."

A page from a long defunct scandal mag. Somehow it had survived the closure of the magazine. Perhaps it had been copied at some stage many years ago onto a server somewhere in the world and never removed.

It was so far down the list that probably no one ever went that far. Certainly Bernard Mayne must have thought it no longer existed or he would have had it removed.

The story was of a dispute between partners of a Ballarat hotel—the Grande Imperial. One of the business partners was accused of cheating the other partners of their share of the profits. While not officially the licensee of the hotel, or even a shareholder whose name appeared in any official accounts, the accused partner had effective control of the hotel and would not pay any returns to his partners. It was also alleged by the disgruntled partners that an illegal gambling house had been set up and run from the hotel. The villain in question was known around the town as Bernie James but his real name was Bernard James Mayne. The shareholders were reluctant to report the gambling to police for fear of losing the hotel licence and had eventually accepted a low payout from some unknown company for their shares. This would confirm the story Suzie had heard from the Kempners. At some stage the gambling had ceased and a new licensee put into the hotel. Mayne had left town at the same time but it was thought by the unhappy investors that the new owner was a nominee company—Chance Nominees No.1—controlled indirectly by Mayne.

We had seen that name before. Chance Nominees No.1 was shown in the Sovereign Group accounts as a 10 per cent interest. Why 10 per cent only Mayne would know. Perhaps he had needed cash and sold an interest to the public company at some stage.

At least that linked Mayne to the Grande when it was used for gambling: even if the police had found nothing. The stories from Wayne and Slowgo had talked of kidnapping of family members of gamblers who didn't meet their debts in

Ballarat. A girl had disappeared and reappeared. From the date that she disappeared it could fit the story, but how would that affect Merry? It still didn't seem to link up unless Billy had gambling debts. We knew he had been to the casino from Roley, and we knew he hadn't paid the local SP bookie in Hamilton. Perhaps he also owed money to Mayne who played rougher than the local SP bookie in collecting his debts. Maybe Merry was picked up in Melbourne. That would fit Slowgo's story of grabbing a girl off the streets of Melbourne. I regretted that I hadn't tried to find out the date that Slowgo had moved to Sydney. Not that I thought he would be forthcoming anyway, but perhaps it could have been significant. But if Merry had been picked up why hadn't she been released?

Then Suzie suddenly stood and left the room. When she came back she had a business card in her hand.

"Can I have another look at the last page of the annual report for Sovereign Group?"

At the end of the Sovereign report there had been a list of offices, legal advisors, banks and similar. One address had seemed familiar to her. It was the Sovereign Group's Hong Kong office.

"I knew I had seen the address before, but I've never been to Hong Kong and I didn't pay any attention to it. Then it came back. It is the address of Roley's office in Hong Kong. It is on the business card he gave me. He must do work for Mayne. Roley must have told Mayne about me. That was when our troubles began, and I thought Roley was harmless."

Suzie's son arrived. As expected he had come as soon as he had been able to get away from work. Max must have taken after his father. He was more solidly built than his mother, with a darker complexion, but he had his mother's eyes. I had suspected from Suzie's remarks that her ex-husband had been good looking and very charming. His son had the looks. I hoped for the sake of Suzie's daughter-in-law he didn't have the same character.

Max was concerned about his mother's car crash. He was especially annoyed at not being told of the details and was worried about her safety. At least he didn't hold me responsible as his sister had done.

Again the suggestion to go to the police. Once more we explained that it wouldn't help. Mayne was a leading city businessman. Sure he may have once owned a hotel in Ballarat that had been raided for gambling but nothing had been found. Sure he may have had white trucks working for him but there were thousands, probably tens of thousands of such trucks in the city. The police had investigated his mother's crash and decided that it was his mother's fault. There was nothing to make a case against Mayne, either regarding his mother or a disappearance many years ago. Any accusations would only look foolish and maybe even make the situation worse. Max agreed.

We had to find more information.

20 BERNARD MAYNE

Peter

Suzie's yellow convertible was going to be at the repair shop for some time. There was a delay caused by some bolt, or nut, or piece of plastic that was not available in Australia and had to be ordered from overseas. It could take weeks. Fortunately her insurance company had agreed to supply a rental vehicle for fourteen days. Hopefully her car would be ready by then. I thought it unlikely, but at least she had a car for two weeks. We decided to pick up the rental.

Suzie also had other plans. She wanted to find out more about Mayne. Where did he live?   She had decided that a man like him would probably live in one of two suburbs of the city so she went online and did a search of phone numbers for Mayne and Toorak. A list of names, numbers and addresses appeared. None had the initial B. Perhaps the phone would be in his wife's name. That still didn't help. All the names that came up lived close to the up-market suburb where Suzie had decided Mayne would probably live, but none of the numbers actually came from that particular suburb. She decided it was probable that his number was unlisted.

Then I remembered many years ago a friend had shown me an electoral roll held in the Mitchell Library in Sydney. It showed a voter's name and address. Mayne would be sure to be on an electoral roll. Perhaps these days the rolls would be online. We searched for the electoral commission. It was possible to check if you were correctly registered on a roll if you used your own name and address, but you could only check the roll for another person by going to an electoral commission office and lodging a complaint that you considered the person to be incorrectly enrolled. We tried a number of possible scenarios to complain about Mayne. Each one seemed unworkable. The problem was we weren't sure we knew his full correct name and we certainly didn't know his address. That was what we were searching for. The electoral office might become suspicious and maybe even contact Mayne. If Mayne really was our problem that would be the last thing we wanted. There was one other option. Apparently electoral rolls up to 2008 were available at some libraries. It would be unlikely that Mayne would change houses and suburbs frequently. Perhaps he would still live in the same house. A house would be a statement like the two door green Rolls we had seen in the photo. From what we had seen on the internet he was the type of personality who would want a grand home as soon as he could afford to make a big statement.

We decided to check out the State Library after we picked up the rental car.

The tiny car the hire company had provided proved a complication. Every city car park we tried was full. We circled for ages trying to find an available space. At last we were able to enter the State Library and begin our search. A helpful guide directed us to the Family History and Newspaper Reading Room. Suzie had spoken of the Reading Room at the Library. She had sometimes visited it when she was studying to be a teacher. The room we walked through was the same octagonal shape but lacked the large high dome that she had described. Nor did the reading desks and chairs scattered throughout the room match her memories of those years. Beyond this room we came to the records we were seeking. A helpful librarian listened to our enquiries and offered solutions. The latest records were not available to the public. Earlier electoral records were available in microfiche however the system had changed. In the last records available all registered voters were listed alphabetically for the entire state. It was not possible to search just an electorate. There could be many Maynes in Victoria. However, if we used records prior to 1990 we could search by electorate. It would be much quicker if Mayne had not moved house in subsequent years. I hoped he didn't keep changing houses.

Our library search paid off. Suzie's hunch on the electorate was correct. In the list for Higgins electorate there was the name, Bernard James Mayne, and an address. There were three other Maynes at the same address. Was it Mayne's wife? Perhaps they were his children? Could it be a son and daughter-in-law? Perhaps a daughter and son-in-law? I thought that unlikely. The daughter would have changed her name on marriage, although as Suzie pointed out my idea was a very old fashioned one. At least we now knew where to find Mayne. We decided to take a drive.

Before we left the Library Suzie took me upstairs to show me the room she had described. Above the octagonal room we had walked through was another room the same shape, but this room was covered by a huge magnificent dome and surrounded by galleries of books. The desks and chairs for readers fanned out in a star shape. The effect was superb.

As Suzie had expected it was a quiet tree-lined street. The grounds were all fronted by high walls and fancy gates. Only the occasional roof showed above the fences. Unlike so many suburbs there were no cars parked on the verge or in the street. Not even tradesmen left their vehicles parked in the street. By the look of the houses there would have to be pool men and gardeners' vehicles somewhere. They must go through the closed gates and be parked on the driveways beyond them. As Suzie drove the baby blue rental car slowly along the street and we searched for the number to locate Mayne's house, a gate opened and a two-tone green Rolls Royce drove out.

"That's Mayne! It's the car we saw in the photo. I'm going to follow him."

Suzie shadowed the big Rolls. I was relaxed. We weren't in a yellow convertible but a tiny pale blue hire car. No one would link us to the car so we would be safe. We wouldn't be recognised.

After fifteen minutes Mayne turned through large open gates and pulled into a carpark. Suzie followed some distance behind and pulled into a parking space away from the Rolls. An elderly grey haired man got out of the green car and walked towards the building.

"He's older than I thought."

Suzie's comment brought home that we had never really given any thought to how old Bernard Mayne would be. Merry had disappeared forty years ago. Mayne had been in business for some time before that, so he could be in his mid-seventies, perhaps even older. The photos on the websites and in the various company reports and articles were either old photos or had been taken by a very flattering photographer. One thing was certain. The only work Mayne was going to do today was on his golf handicap.

When we returned to Suzie's house she decided to try Google Earth to see if she could look at Mayne's house. Now that we had the address it was easy to locate. The street view showed the fence and the elegant heavy wooden gates we had seen earlier in the afternoon. From the look of neighbouring houses Mayne must have bought two blocks of land and demolished the earlier houses. With his contacts in the building industry he had been able to build his dream house.

The man had good taste. It was a large two-storey white building with floor to ceiling glass windows looking out onto the garden and pool. Perhaps there was a touch of art deco in the design but in a much more modern expression. From the look of the house Mayne had found a great architect to design his home. Being set back from the street, nothing of the house could be seen from the street. The driveway from the elegant wooden gates led to the front of the house and a parking area, from there it continued along the side of the house to a ramp leading down to the basement. The garage must be down there. At the rear of the house a patio overlooked a large swimming pool. A tennis court shared the matching pool house. The grounds were landscaped with mature trees, walkways and a manicured garden. Mayne certainly enjoyed all the home comforts his success could buy.

"I want to have another look at the house. Let's go for another drive past it."

I thought Suzie's suggestion unnecessary and tried to talk her out of going, but she was insistent. I asked why she wanted to go.

"I just have a feeling about it. I backed your hunch in Ballarat. Now you can back mine."

Unlike Suzie I had a bad feeling about returning to Mayne's house. I was sure we would gain nothing. We wouldn't see anything because of the high fence and the solid gates, but Suzie remained insistent, and there was no way I could talk her out of going. Again the pale blue car drove slowly down the tree-lined street. As we passed Mayne's gate a small security camera mounted high on the wall swung around and followed our path.

21 THE NOTE

Suzie

Peter was not happy when we returned from our second drive past Mayne's house. He had let me know that we were pushing our luck driving past the second time. He became even more annoyed when I made a joke about 'casing the joint'. Peter had taken the remark seriously and been quite sharp in his response. When I attempted to play down the joke he became even more annoyed. I decided it would be better not to discuss that subject anymore. He was still in a quiet, tense mood when I pulled 'Baby Blue', as I had christened the hire car, into the driveway of my home.

I decided to offer him some fresh cooked scones with jam and cream and a cup of tea. Hopefully that might lift his grumpy mood. My mother had always told me a way to a man's heart was through his stomach, then she would pointedly look at my father. I wondered, did I really want Peter's heart?

There was obviously something troubling him, but what it was I had no idea. Nor did I think Peter was likely to open up about his concerns if I questioned him. I would just have to wait until he was ready to talk.

The smell from the kitchen must have had an effect. Peter's mood seemed to lighten. We decided to sit on the little patio beside the kitchen door, catch the last of the sun and enjoy our scones and tea. I think I would have preferred a glass of sav blanc at this time of day, but I had made the scones and they appeared to be working. While we were drinking our tea a black ute drove slowly up the street, stopped across the road from us, and put the window down. It was a fancy looking ute. The type that appeals to cashed up tradies who deck their vehicles out with fancy expensive hubs, wide wheels and powerful motors. It was all black with dark tinted windows and not a glint of chrome anywhere. It was difficult to be sure, but from where we were sitting it appeared that the driver was taking a photo of my house, then he drove off.

I looked at Peter.

"What was that about?"

"Someone likes the look of your house. Perhaps they want to buy it or design something along the same lines. Either that, or your friends are still keeping an eye on you."

"What should we do?"

"Act innocent. Pretend we are not interested. We haven't noticed. Don't give them any reason for concern. Don't ask any questions. I think that is all we can do at present."

I was beginning to admit to myself that perhaps Peter was right after all. It may not have been a good idea to drive past Mayne's house the second time. However I was not going to give up on what had happened to Merry, regardless of what Peter thought best.

I had been going to suggest that we visit a little Thai restaurant for dinner. It was not far from my house and usually had a noisy fun atmosphere. However I sensed that Peter was still not in a mood that would make dining out a pleasure. Perhaps it would be better if I cooked something for dinner and we ate in. Again my mother's comment came to mind. I decided to do my favourite recipe, a chicken and apricot casserole. At least I would enjoy it. I had no idea if it would suit Peter but I couldn't accuse myself of using it as way to his heart. While I was cooking Emma phoned. She was to fly to Adelaide the next day for a conference and wanted to check up on me before leaving. Fortunately Peter was watching the evening news on the television in the next room. Emma's opposition to Peter had only hardened. I didn't see any possibility of her accepting Peter.

"This is delicious."

From the way it had disappeared off the plate Peter obviously enjoyed my favourite dish.

After we had finished our meal we moved to the lounge room where Peter poured drinks, the usual scotch for himself and brandy and dry for me. At last he opened up. He was concerned about our arrangement. What was it? Were we just friends sharing a bed or were we lovers? If we were lovers where were we going? He didn't see himself moving in with me but would I want to move to Sydney with him?

The thought of leaving Melbourne and moving to Sydney did not appeal to me. My children and my grandchild were in Melbourne. My friends were in Melbourne. I knew no one in Sydney. Besides, this was my home. I liked my independence. I could see my thoughts would hurt Peter.

But then I liked being with him. As serious as he could sometimes be, he was a great companion and I really enjoyed his company. Even the sex was special. I realised it was something I had missed for many years. Perhaps we could split our time between houses. Peter pointed out the impracticalities of living nine hundred kilometres apart. Besides he did not want that. That was like the fly-in/fly-out life that stressed so many of the relationships he had seen with his workmates. He knew what it was like and did not want it again. If he committed it would have to be all the way. He was not interested in a casual affair.

He also hated the feeling of being a kept man. Suddenly I realised why he always insisted on paying every time we went to a supermarket or fruit shop. I would go to pay, thinking he was my guest and it was my hospitality, but he would brush my card aside and pay. I wondered if the situation would be reversed if I was visiting in Sydney. I suspected he would still not want me to pay, or let me pay, and he would insist on being the generous host. How would we arrange matters if we lived together? He really was an old fashioned man. I think my father would have approved of him.

We decided that he would return to Sydney and I would fly up in a few weeks and spend time with him. We would see what happened. I don't think Peter was entirely happy but he agreed. I was very unsure of my decision but I realised I did want to spend time with him. Neither of us went to bed confident of our decisions.

I had talked Peter into taking a walk with me in the morning. I always enjoyed my walks before breakfast. It seemed to set me up for the day and I loved listening to the birds coming alive as I walked through the park. Every day was different and I used to do it most mornings unless the weather was bad.

As we returned to the house there was a white van pulled up one house away from mine but on the opposite side of the street. It looked like the type of van a TV serviceman would use, or perhaps a repairman for a phone company. As we looked at it a black ute drove up and the driver of the van got out, got into the black ute and the ute drove away. The van driver was another big, heavily tattooed man. I wasn't sure but the ute looked like the same one we had seen yesterday afternoon.

Peter grabbed me and stopped me from walking on. We waited until the black ute had disappeared around the corner. We stood watching for another five minutes but there was no movement or sound coming from the vehicle. We approached the white van cautiously. The windows were tinted black and it was difficult to see through the rear or side windows. We moved to the front of the van and looked through the front window. It was empty. There appeared to be some box-like arrangement sitting on a bench and taped to the window facing my house. A cable ran from the box to a laptop computer sitting on the same bench. Peter decided it was probably a video camera. Whether it was simply recording or sending the pictures to a remote watcher over the mobile phone system he couldn't say. Being aimed at my house it would not have filmed us looking into the van.

"Let's go back to the corner of the street. Cross over the other side and walk back to the house. If they are videoing us they will see us come and not know that we have picked up their ploy. They will just think we are coming back from a walk. I wonder if it also does infra-red at night."

The presence of the van meant somebody is very interested in what we are doing. Our enquiries at the State Library would not have attracted attention. The librarian would have no idea whose name we were checking. It was unlikely that our internet searches would have tipped anyone off, so it must have been the two trips past Mayne's house. They had seen the blue car, perhaps their camera had even seen me driving. If not that then perhaps it was a just a random check on me from the earlier surveillance and they had seen the blue car in my driveway. That had caused them to pay more attention to me. Was the van just for surveillance or was it also meant as a threat? The white van changed Peter's plans. He no longer wanted to fly back to Sydney but decided to stay with me.

The threat posed by the van made me want to do something. Perhaps it was time to go to the police, but could we find a definite reason? The white van might be a reason but I could imagine the incredulity of the local officers if we said that someone was spying on us. They would probably not be concerned unless the van showed up on a list of stolen vehicles and it would need to sit for much longer before it was considered dumped. At best they might drive past, and if they bothered to stop and look in all they would see was a computer and a box. In any case we were sure the van would not be linked to Mayne. He would be too clever to allow that.

While we were having breakfast Amelia and Charles arrived. Max had no doubt suggested to his wife that she meet Peter. Charlie immediately took to Peter. I remember Peter saying his son, while having no children of his own, was a favourite honorary uncle to many of his friend's children. I could see Peter as being a favourite granddad.

Charlie had already made his decision and, unlike Emma, Amelia was much more receptive to Peter. While I made coffee they chatted happily together. I could see Amelia reporting favourably to her husband. As they left I remembered the white van and its camera. No doubt it had recorded their visit.

Over another cup of coffee we reviewed our situation. We were getting nowhere. We had no answers and no facts, only suspicions, and now our watchers were back. Hayman had not thrown them off our case. Our thoughts were just going around endlessly in a circle without ever finding any answers.

"I have trouble with all the ideas floating around in my mind. I know we have gone over it time and time again but let's do it one more time."

Peter agreed and suggested that this time we write our thoughts down on paper. It might help. At least he seemed to be on my side again.

I commenced.

"We know Billy was a gambler, probably losing money at a casino in Ballarat according to Roley. The casino was run by a man who later went on to be a big businessman. Mayne started out in Ballarat and became a leading businessman so it fitted Mayne, but could have been someone else.

Mayne's first business in Melbourne was Grande Developments. He could also have been involved with the Grande Imperial but the only link we have is the font style in the similar names and the suspected link to Chance Nominees No.1. So the circumstantial evidence points to Mayne."

Peter agreed.

"According to your Sydney friend the man running the gambling had a habit of using muscle and kidnapping to collect debts. We didn't know if the girl who disappeared and reappeared may have had a connection to the gambling. Merry disappeared so that could have been in keeping with the pattern if Billy had a debt to Mayne."

Peter agreed that it was a possible scenario.

"Billy had a car crash, I was run off the road and had a crash. That could have happened to Billy."

This time Peter disagreed.

"Billy was obviously driving very fast. It was a dark wet night. From his mother's comments he was upset when he left Oakleigh. He certainly wasn't relaxed. I think it was just an accident. Who would have known he was on that road at that time? I doubt if he would have been followed from Oakleigh. It just seems too unlikely. Besides why kill him? You can't collect money from a dead man."

"Then you don't think my accident was arranged? I assure you it was! They could have killed me. If you didn't think they were serious why the trip to Hayman? Was it just a way to get me in the cot?"

"No it was not! To get you into the cot, I mean! I agree your accident was pre-arranged. I just don't think Billy's was. Our, your, trouble started after Ballarat and you also had the warning about asking questions."

"So who would be interested in us?"

"It must have been someone we spoke to or somewhere we

have been."

"The publican of the Grande Imperial?"

"Why? We were no threat to him. Unless he passed on our interest to someone else? Possibly Mayne still owns the freehold of the pub. He at least appears to have some interest in it. Then you had lunch with Roley. He knew who ran the casino, he had been there and seen Billy. Perhaps he was also losing and as a lawyer did the boss a few favours. It looks like he still does work for Mayne. He could have told Mayne about your questions."

"What about your friends in Sydney. Could they have tipped off Mayne or whoever is behind it?"

"Slowgo couldn't have told them about you as I didn't mention your name, or even mine for that matter. I just said I was a friend of Wayne's. He didn't know either of our names although I suppose he could have passed on a message that someone was asking questions. He is the sort of bloke who would do that if he thought there were a few dollars in it for him. Even then I doubt anyone would link an enquiry in Sydney with interest in Melbourne, or to you, so it must have been Ballarat or Melbourne. In any case they must have been watching you in order to try to run you off the road. I agree it all seems to lead to the gambling but still doesn't link it to Mayne conclusively."

I thought of my comment about casing the joint. Perhaps Peter felt we may have to break into Mayne's house. I shuddered at the thought as I remembered the security camera on the wall. I was sure the house would be well protected. It was after we drove past Mayne's house that we got the visit from the black ute, and now we had the white van parked opposite. That would seem to be a link. If the camera had seen the blue car drive past twice, and then Mayne's man in the black ute had seen the same blue car parked in my driveway, he would realise we were suspicious of him.

It is still hardly enough to take to the police.

"Well, how about this."

I started to write a list.

Grande Imperial—gambling.

Billy owes money.

Mayne threatens, kidnaps Billy's sister (Merry). Billy rushes to Ballarat to sort out problem. Perhaps to ask for more time.

Billy killed in an accident, Merry was also killed to hide any connection.

Mayne finds out about questions being asked—from publican? Roley?

Finds my address, arranges accident to silence me.

We drive past house, he, or someone, recognises car, watches my house again.

We are back in danger.

"How does that look to you?"

"Well it's possible, but it is all just circumstantial, and I don't see the bit about the two murders. That's not the way to collect a debt."

"Perhaps it was a warning to others to pay up or else."

"For that to work others would have to know. Nothing has ever come out after all these years. If Merry was murdered then it was kept very quiet."

"Your mate, Slowgo, was shunted off to Sydney very quickly. Could that have anything to do with it if he had picked up Merry?"

"Perhaps. He did say he and another man picked up a girl in Melbourne and took her to Ballarat, but he didn't say when. Then he left Ballarat. He hasn't had any contact with the other man or the boss since then. I don't think he would tell me about it anyway. Maybe he would talk to the police if they picked him up. From the way he spoke I gathered the girl was still alive when he left. He never spoke of any deaths, although you would hardly expect him to say anything."

"Where did he take the girl?"

"To Ballarat. To a building near the hotel. That was all he said. I can't see them holding a prisoner in the hotel. It would be too public. It would have to be some other place."

"Roley told me that the gambling was somewhere underground. You went into the hotel and then went down and along a tunnel to a large room, like a big basement. Perhaps there were rooms underground."

"The same thing. You would hardly keep a prisoner next to your gambling room. Although the girl who was released reported she was in a room without windows and it was cold. That could be a cellar."

"Perhaps something went wrong. Billy couldn't pay. He may not have had the money. That's quite possible. He would have had plenty of spending money but not access to big sums. I think he was good at spending every penny he earned fairly quickly. Even if he had found some money he never got to Ballarat to pay Mayne because of the accident. What would have happened to Merry?"

As I asked the question I was already answering it to myself. They couldn't let her go. She was sure to report her kidnapping to the police. That would be the end of their business and probably jail. She would hold them responsible for her brother's death and that would make her even more determined to get justice. I could see how my old friend would react. They would have no way of silencing her short of murder.

I wrote on my note. Mayne murdered her!

It still wasn't enough to take to the police. Peter suggested we leave it one more day and if the van remained we would go to the police. Until then he would stay with me.

22 THE BREAK-IN

Suzie

The day had been unsettling. The white van remained parked across the street from my house. We had made no progress in deciding on a course of action. Both of us were uneasy and tense. I needed to buy food and Peter wanted to buy a newspaper, so we drove to the local shopping centre. It was late in the afternoon when we returned from the supermarket. As before, I left 'Baby Blue' parked in the driveway. The white van had gone. Further down the street a green car was parked under the shade of a tree. I wondered whether we had lost our surveillance, or whether we had just had a change of shift and now had a new watcher. When we entered the house Peter stopped and looked around the room. I was puzzled by his behaviour. He raised his finger to his lips and motioned me to be silent. Then, strangely, he started to talk about the supermarket. All the time he was looking around the room for something. At last he found a pencil and an old shopping list in the kitchen and he scribbled a note.

Someone's been here. Pretend you don't know. Talk normally but don't say anything important.

I stood, not knowing what to say or what to do. He quickly checked the main rooms in the house and came back, turned on the television then started talking about the football match on the screen.

He scribbled another note.

Someone has been here while we were out. I think the books on the side-table have been moved. I left them at angles and now they are straight.

Then he spoke. "Could you make me a cup of coffee please?"

"Filter or expresso?" I humoured him.

"Expresso would be great."

Again I went silent and made two coffees. At least this time the television provided a background of noise. Peter continued his search, more thoroughly this time, throughout the whole house, room by room. He came back and continued to talk about the football as he wrote a longer note.

My suitcase has also been searched. Everything is where it was but not in quite the same way—just a little different. The house has been searched thoroughly. I expect it was our friends across the road or someone they know. Just act as if we don't know but don't say anything about Mayne in case we are bugged.

I wrote back. *Who is being paranoid now?*

Our conversation took a strange double pattern. We spoke of trivial things, comments about the football match, and scribbled meaningful notes to each other.

"You are the Melbourne girl. Who do you think will win this game?"

He wrote, *It would be easy to do. There is so much gear available in the electronic shops these days. I hope they haven't put in a camera as well.*

"I haven't been following it much this year."

You really are being paranoid! I scribbled back.

"I don't follow AFL. I'm Sydney born and bred so I follow rugby."

They must think, or at least be afraid, that we know something. But what? We have nothing. Suspicions yes, but facts, no. What are they worried about?

"Max has taken me to a few games. He follows Hawthorn."

Do you think we are in danger? I wrote.

"How did you enjoy the atmosphere at the game?"

It seems to be getting worse. At first I thought the attempt to run you off the road was a warning. At least it would distract you from making any enquiries if you ended up in hospital. I don't think it was designed to kill you although that could have been a plus for them, it would have removed any further risk.

Thank you for your kind thoughts! I scribbled back.

Our continued interest when we drove past Mayne's house a second time must have alerted them again. Maybe it was the security camera and then seeing 'Baby Blue' parked in the driveway. They, he, whoever, must be really worried to make the effort to break in. It just creates more complications.

Do you think he broke in?

As I wrote it I realised that I couldn't envisage the old man we had seen at the golf course sneaking into my house and searching it.

No, I don't see him as a burglar, but I suspect he would have contacts who could arrange it. If we don't know anything then we shouldn't be in any danger. I don't think he would want to have two unexplained murder enquiries if there was no need. All the same I think we need to be very careful. I don't think he would stop if he thought it necessary.

What do we do? I wrote back.

Stay calm. Pretend we haven't noticed. Do you have the notes you wrote when we were doing the internet searches on Mayne?

"They're not here! I put them in my address book beside the bed. I'm sure I did. They're not there. They've gone!"

In my haste and concern I had spoken out rather than written.

Peter was quick to realise my mistake.

"I thought you put the cards with the dentist's number in your wallet. You were going to put it in your address book but you changed your mind because you thought you would ring for an appointment when we were out for a coffee."

Peter suddenly grabbed the paper and pencil and started to write.

Was that the piece of paper we had written our ideas on, with the information about Mayne?

"Yes."

Including saying that he was responsible for Merry's death.

"Yes."

Then if he gets it, and he was responsible, we are in deep trouble. I'm worried. I think we should take precautions, and quickly!

23 THE FIRE

Suzie

The early morning television news carried the report.

"Police are this morning investigating a house fire in the Melbourne suburb of Armadale.

"Fire brigades were called to the scene in Bolton Avenue, Armadale at eleven thirty last night by neighbours who heard a loud explosion and found the house blazing furiously. So far the investigators have failed to locate the occupants, believed to be a man and a woman.

"Police are treating the fire as suspicious and are asking for any persons who saw any activity in the area to contact Crimestoppers on 1800 333 000.

"Neighbours described the owner as an elderly woman who had lived in the house for around ten years, and was a quiet neighbour with an interest in gardening.

"Preliminary investigations indicate the fire is suspicious but unlikely to be caused by an illegal drug laboratory or connected to the recent spate of drug related incidents and shootings.

"Police are still searching the remains of the house but have so far been unable to recover any bodies."

24 TRAPPED

Peter

The white van was a sign we hadn't convinced our 'friends' that we weren't a threat. My hope that they would stop watching us after our return from Hayman Island had obviously not worked. I certainly did not want another attempt on Suzie's life.

With the break-in they knew we believed Mayne was responsible for Merry's death. If he had killed her then he would hardly be worried about what happened to us, just as long as it couldn't be linked to him. I was sure both our lives were now in danger. We needed to disappear, and disappear fast.

The answer must be in Ballarat, so perhaps that would be a good hiding place. They would hardly expect us to go there, and we may be able to follow up one more lead.

I was still worried that the house might be bugged; it would be so easy to do. I suggested to Suzie that we take a walk to the park before it became dark. That way we could make our plans without any risk of being overheard. The green car was still parked in the same place. As we approached the driver moved his eyes away from the rear vision mirror to a newspaper open in front of him. When we returned from our walk he was still watching us while pretending to read the paper, even though the light was rapidly fading.

Our plan was to leave as soon as it became sufficiently dark. We were in luck with the weather. It was overcast with heavy grey clouds and no moon. It would be a black night. I would arrange for some house lights and the sound system to be activated by timers. Once it was dark I would take the car down to the nearby takeaway and pick up some food plus a bottle of champagne from the liquor store on my way back to the house. I hoped it would look to any watcher that we were planning a romantic evening at home. All the front exterior lights of the house would be on and Suzie would wave me goodbye, reminding me loudly not to forget the champagne. I would delay my departure by getting out of the car and looking for something in the boot giving Suzie time to re-enter the house, draw the blinds and then sneak out the back door, which would be in darkness, climb over the back fence into the neighbour's yard and wait for me two streets away. The neighbours would probably be watching television and unlikely to see her sneak past. I hoped that anyone watching the house would be concentrating on me and not notice her departure.

On my return I would put on the music and switch on the timers so it would appear we were eating, listening to music and finally heading to the bedroom, then I would slip away through the backdoor to join her.

I would text her when I was preparing to leave the house. Suzie would order a taxi and we would go to my friends in Mont Albert. I was sure I would be able to borrow Rob's second car for a few days. If anyone was watching we would hopefully be in Ballarat by the time the bedroom lights turned off.

Roley had told Suzie the entrance to the gambling club was through a tunnel from the hotel. That seemed to cross out any adjoining buildings. They would only require a hole in the wall. The building behind the hotel was also unlikely because of the topography. The hotel was on the corner of a major street and a narrow lane which would have once provided access to the original hotel stables. He had said there was a tunnel under the road. Was it the wide street or the lane? He had spoken confidently to Suzie in describing the access to the gaming room and he seemed the sort of person who would have a sense of direction. If the tunnel went under the narrow lane it would have been very short, and I felt that it wouldn't really have created much impact as a tunnel. On the other hand a tunnel under the wide road would have registered with the patrons. It could even add an atmosphere of theatre to visiting the gaming room. However it couldn't be too long as some people might become uneasy being underground in a confined space. I decided the gambling venue was probably across the wide street.

I was still puzzled by how close such a tunnel would be to the road surface, but while discussing the problem as we drove to Ballarat the dilemma was resolved. Roley had told Suzie that you went down steps into the tunnel. Suzie had thought that meant stairs in the hotel. However she and Merry had watched people enter the lift and disappear. If the lift went down to the basement and the patrons then went down more stairs after they left the lift that would put a greater thickness of material between the top of the tunnel and the road above. I had a second puzzle as well. Although I knew the city was riddled with tunnels from mining, they would be much deeper. Then I remembered that some mines were entered by an incline rather than a shaft. This would start at surface level and gradually go deeper. Our tunnel could be part of an old incline. With all the spoil from the excavations and mullock heaps the original ground level had probably changed dramatically as well. This would also affect the height of the road above the tunnel.

Diagonally opposite the hotel, to the right, were a church and a church hall. I couldn't see Mayne conducting card games in the crypt so that was out. Opposite, to the left, beside the lane, were two single-storey, narrow-fronted office buildings. If they had basements they would be too small to meet the description Roley had given Suzie. That left the building directly opposite. It was a large two-storey office building. I was sure it would have a large basement. Even better it was derelict. The wall was daubed with 'Stop the demolition. Save our heritage.' The main entrance to the building had solid wooden shutters fitted in front of what would have once been an ornate entry in keeping with the style of building. The windows' original wrought iron guards, with their peeling paint, were still in place and a street light shone covering the front of the building in light. Not a place for two amateur detectives—or burglars. The side of the building on the lane was in shadow and the lane appeared unused. It certainly offered a better prospect, particularly as the windows were not guarded by wrought iron but only by wooden boards nailed or screwed into the window frames.

We had come prepared. Black can be a very fashionable colour. However it is also commonly thought to be the classic colour for burglars. Even in a black skivvy and slacks, rather than a little black dress, Suzie still retained her touch of style and looked an unlikely burglar. My dark jumper and trousers didn't have the same elegance.

With the jemmy and large screwdriver which I had borrowed from my friend I had my breaking and entering equipment. I hoped it would be sufficient. When I had made my request to Rob he had queried my need for the gear, and when I told him the truth—that I may want to break into a building—he had given me a very puzzled look.

We loitered by the window like a pair of love birds until we were sure we were unobserved. Then I went to work. The boards were nailed into the window frames so it only took a minute to prise away enough for an opening to allow me through. The bigger problem was smashing the glass and clearing it away so we could climb in without cutting ourselves in the process. I thought next time I do this I must bring something to cover the glass, but that might leave clues for the police.

The street was deserted as I lifted Suzie up so she could crawl through the broken window, and then I clambered in after her.

We were in what had once been an office. A desk and empty bookcase still occupied the room. Seeing an old pin board lying against the wall I jammed it across the broken window, hoping that if anyone looked it would seem like a cheap repair of the broken glass. With my hand shielding the light from my small torch we opened the door. It led into a hallway. At the far end stairs went up to the next floor, beside them another set went down to what would be the basement. If you entered a building through a tunnel, under a road, then that was where we needed to look. We cautiously moved down the hallway. Unbeknown to us a little yellow light, mounted high on the wall behind us, changed to red.

The stairs wound down more than the usual thickness between floors. The basement held several small rooms which would have once been store rooms and another room, with an old fashioned steel safe, that may have been an office. There were two rather fancy toilets labelled 'Gentlemen' and 'Ladies'. Another short flight of stairs opened into the main room. This was different. It was large, but it was the decor that stood out. While the paint was old it had once been a dark red with an ornate trim of cream and gold. One corner of the room had a long counter that could have been a bar when the room was in use. There was a multitude of cords hanging from the ceiling. All the shades had gone and only a few of the cords still had bulbs attached. The only furniture was a few old chairs, some of them broken. It was hard to think of this drab, empty, windowless room filled with high stakes gamblers.

In our torchlight we could see a heavy gilt trimmed door at the far end of the room. It obviously led somewhere, and from its position I suspected it must be the tunnel to the Grande Imperial. We went across the room to the door. It opened with a squeak. Behind it was a smaller room, possibly an ante room or cloak room, again another door, smaller and not as ornate. Beyond this door we found the tunnel.

Patches of dull white on the walls showed signs of the tunnel once having been white-washed, but now it had faded to a mottled grey and dirty white. In the torchlight we could see where there were lights along its length. From the cobwebs on the walls the tunnel had had little use, or care, for many years.

A number of tunnels ran off either side in various places. Some had been closed off with heavy iron doors, on others the iron doors were open. In the torchlight we couldn't see where they ended as they sloped off deeper underground.

The narrow beam of my torch lit up the tunnel ahead as we passed one of these side leads.

"Stop, hands on the wall or I will shoot!"

We were suddenly in the harsh light of a powerful torch which appeared to come from the side tunnel we had just passed.

"Lie on the ground, face down, now! I have a gun!"

I started to ask what this was about but didn't even get to finish.

"Down! Now!" The tone didn't suggest discussion was possible.

The tunnel was only about two metres wide so by the time I was lying stretched out I covered the width of the tunnel. Suzy lay beside me. In the light from the torch I could see her looking at me with a puzzled expression on her face.

The voice from the side tunnel came closer. "If you move I will shoot!" The tone of the voice left no doubt that he meant it. The voice was familiar. It was our surly barman from the hotel. The torch beam wavered and came back onto us spreadeagle on the floor. I could feel the presence of the gunman just inches away from me as he emerged from his hiding place. Then I heard the taps. I couldn't place the sound until I realised he was using a mobile phone. I wondered whether he would have reception underground, but then we were not that far under a road, no buildings would be above us and we were in the centre of town so there could be some reception. There was a pause and what seemed to be an answer. Lying on the floor we could only hear one side of the conversation. Our capturer reported finding us and obviously was asked to describe us. He seemed to be given instructions but what they were we couldn't tell. We heard our gunman say, "Here", a pause, "Now," another pause and then there seemed to be a long set of orders. It didn't sound good, especially when he asked which tunnel.

The torch seemed to wave around and I thought if he has a gun, a torch and is using a phone he will have his hands full. Perhaps he doesn't have a gun. His tone of voice and the threats would seem to count that out as an option, and I certainly didn't want to rely on him bluffing. Probably he was holding the torch with his arm or shoulder while he was using one hand for the phone and the other for the gun. Once he finished talking and put the phone away he would be able to concentrate fully on us. If we are to have a chance it must be now while he is still on the phone. A few more seconds and it could be too late.

I touched Suzie on the arm, hoping to warn her to be prepared, and then I suddenly pushed back with my hands and lashed out with my feet. I felt the thud as I connected with his legs and felt him stumble backwards. The torch fell to the floor and went out. I wasn't sure whether the dark would be an advantage but at least it made us even. I twisted sideways and gained my feet. I stayed low. The shot was deafening in the confined space. If I had been standing it would have hit me but it just smashed into the wall where we had first stood. We now knew he wasn't bluffing about the gun but the flash showed him up and I lunged at him catching him at waist height. We stumbled back into the side tunnel. I heard a metallic sound as something fell on the floor. I hoped it was the gun. In the dark neither of us could see the other so it became a wrestling match in which neither would give way. I could hear Suzie scrabbling in the dark but had no idea what she was doing.

It seemed to be ages that we wrestled together. I thought from my rush at him and the feel when I bumped against walls that we were pushing into the side tunnel. I was probably deeper into the tunnel than our gunman. I almost tripped on Suzie. She seemed to be squatting on the floor. I hoped the bullet hadn't ricocheted and hit her. She must have moved behind me and be even deeper into the tunnel.

I should have been concentrating on my assailant. I was in agony. He had kneed me in my crotch. With the pain I released my grip and I felt him break away. The next moment there was a clang as the heavy iron door of the side tunnel shut. I lunged at the door but it was too late. I heard the bolt slide home. We were locked in.

I felt a hand touch my leg. It was Suzie.

"Are you alright?" I could hear the concern in her whispered enquiry.

"Where is he?"

Beside her whisper my reply seemed a hollow bellow in the tunnel.

"He must be outside, on the other side of the door, to be able to lock it. I can't feel any catch on this side."

A small light appeared. Suzie still had her torch. Mine

must be lying on the floor somewhere.

"At least he doesn't have the gun. I heard it drop and I found it on the floor. I didn't want to use the torch because I didn't know if it would be a help or a hindrance for you. I couldn't use the gun. You were both so close together."

With the torch we inspected the door. The heavy steel door must have dated from the mining in the late eighteen hundreds or the early twentieth century. The initial inspection was correct. There was no catch on our side. The door was evidently designed to shut the side tunnel off from the main tunnel and must have bolted from that side. We were trapped.

At least we did have a torch and a gun, and a phone. Lying on the ground near the door was a mobile phone. It must have been dropped in the fight. Feeling my pocket I still had mine.

"Is that your phone?"

"No."

It seemed we not only had our assailant's gun but also his phone. We could check who he had last called. The only problem was his phone no longer worked. It must have been damaged when it hit the floor. Nor would our phones work. We must have been on the very edge of reception and now our carrier was out of range.

At least we had the gun. I checked it out. We had five bullets left.

"What happens now?"

Suzie's question focused me on our future. There seemed

to be a number of choices. Perhaps he was waiting outside. That didn't seem likely. He didn't have his gun. He didn't know we had it but it would still worry him, anyway he had us locked in. He could come back, probably with another gun if he had one. I didn't like the thought of a shootout. Maybe he would bring a mate, or his boss. That would be worse. He could just walk away and leave us to die of starvation. Nobody would come looking for us here. I hadn't told Rob where we were going. He would become concerned when we didn't return his car but would have no idea where we may have gone, especially with tools for burglary.

None of the choices were good. We had to get out and get out fast. Since we couldn't go out the door we only had one way to go. With Suzie's torch we worked our way down the tunnel. It appeared to be slowly but steadily sloping downwards. Unlike the main tunnel the side leads didn't have doors, although several had boards across them to stop entry. Most were open and the torchlight showed them as smaller than the tunnel we were in. From the way they led off in an irregular manner I suspected they were following old gold leads. None appeared to offer a way out.

One side branch was different. While the others were closed off with boards or left open this one was blocked by rocks. There had been a few rocks lying along the floor in the tunnel we were in and we had seen small heaps of stones in the side tunnels. This was different. A rough wall had been built across the entrance and the rocks set in concrete. Whoever built the wall had wanted to stop people using that particular lead. They had also been in a hurry as the wall was poorly built.

As the torch played over the wall and floor a sudden glint of something on the floor caught our attention. My shoes had disturbed the dust and dirt and something was lying on the floor. Suzie bent down and picked it up. She shuddered and I saw her eyes widen. In her hand she held a gold bracelet. The safety chain was broken.

"This is Merry's."

"What do you mean?"

"I know this bracelet. I gave it to Merry for her twenty-first birthday. It had a little charm of a koala on it. Look here. Why is it here?"

If the bracelet was here, Merry, or someone who had taken the bracelet from her, must have been here. Suddenly the rocks blocking the side tunnel became ominous. That the chain was broken suggested a struggle. If someone had stolen it from her why would it be here? The thought that came to mind was worrying. For Suzie's sake I hoped I was wrong. Frantically I started pulling at a few rocks that looked weaker than the rest. This is where my jemmy and large screwdriver would have been handy, but they were back in the main tunnel and the man could be returning with another gun and helpers. At last one rock came free and I was able to get more purchase and free another. Soon we had opened up a small hole and could shine the torch through to see what the builder had wanted hidden.

As I feared there was a body, but there was not just one body but two. Both were slumped against the side wall of the short tunnel as if they had been just thrown in like discarded waste. From the dress covering the remains one was a woman, the other, from the jumper, the trousers, the lace-up leather shoes and size probably a man—a very big man. The first body I had feared, the second was a puzzle.

Suzie looked and I saw her start to cry. "It's Merry. I remember that dress. It was a favourite. She used to wear it to work quite often."

I took her in my arms and held her. I could feel her body shaking with her tears. Eventually she moved free and looked at me in the torchlight. "I guess that answers the mystery. Now we know."

Merry's disappearance had been solved. We had found her. The bracelet must have come off in a struggle or when her body was being placed in its tomb. In the darkness the murderer had not seen it when he hurriedly closed up the entrance. Probably the other body was the Ox, Slowgo's mate, who had stayed behind in Ballarat and had never been seen again. The size of the body would fit the description Dot had given of her missing brother. It would explain the disappearance of Frank O'Hartigan, but it also meant the murderer was someone else. It was hardly likely to be our assailant from earlier in the night. He was far too young for the murders of forty years ago. Probably it was his boss, the man he spoke to on the phone. The man who had ordered the accident with Suzie's car. With two old murders and another two attempted tonight he would have a very good reason to want us to disappear forever.

"We have to get out of here. We must keep looking. There may be another entrance or another shaft. Perhaps we will find a spot where the phones work."

I noticed Suzie was shivering. I thought it was the shock of finding her friend's body and then I realised it wasn't just her. I was feeling colder. As you go deeper underground the temperature rises and in deep shafts the workers can get very hot. In a tunnel like this, which was not very deep but closed up, the ground above would isolate the tunnel from outside temperature changes. There had to be air coming in from outside. Above, it would be just before dawn and the coldest part of the night. That must mean an entrance or an airshaft. It wasn't behind us or we would have seen or felt it. It was unlikely to be in the smaller side tunnels so it must be ahead.

"We must move! Our friend will be back. The man behind all this won't want his secret to get out. Keep checking the roof as well, there may be an air vent or a shaft for taking out ore."

25 TRAPPED AGAIN

Peter

The tunnel we were now in was lower than the one which we had first entered from the derelict building. In the torchlight the offshoot tunnels appeared even lower and narrower. Nor were they as straight as our tunnel but seemed to twist and bend, sometimes coming to an abrupt halt, at other times turning out of the flashlight's beam. I thought of the old miners, working with little light, following the veins of gold that promised so much but often gave so little for their efforts. The walls and roofs of these side leads were much more roughly hewn and their floors not as level as the floor of the tunnel we were in. Years ago I guess this tunnel would have seen much more traffic. The floor, which had been sloping down ever since we had entered, now seemed to have a little less slope. I estimated we had gone down about six or eight metres from our break and enter window to the start of this tunnel. Since then we had continued to go deeper into the ground but I had no idea how much deeper. In any case I had no knowledge of the topography of the earth over us. The ground level above may have risen up in a hill, or dropped away and we could still be close to the surface.

I hoped this tunnel would lead to an exit. In that case we would have to come out at the side of a hill, alternatively there could be a shaft that would have been used to remove ore. The materials from these tunnels must have been taken somewhere for processing and to eventually end up on a mullock heap. Another option would be an airshaft but there was no way of knowing how deep that shaft would be or how we could get up it. Perhaps we could get mobile signal and call for help if we stood at the bottom of the shaft. First we had to find a shaft or exit.

"The entrance isn't behind us so it must be ahead. We must keep walking, and I think we had better hurry. I don't want to be in here if our friend returns."

We continued our stumbling torchlight progress along the tunnel, tripping on the occasional unseen rocks poking from the floor. Eventually the tunnel seemed to increase in size and the floor became flatter and more even. Now it also had parallel ruts carved into it. That was a good sign. Wagons must have once been pushed or dragged along it. Whether by man, or perhaps pit ponies, made no difference. The ore must have passed this way because there had been no sign of the tracks when we had first entered the tunnel.

It was hard to measure the distance we had travelled in the tunnel but I thought maybe eight hundred metres. My estimate could be very inaccurate, and I only had a rough idea of the direction we had travelled. I was sure of the direction of the tunnel between the building we had broken into and the hotel, but since then the tunnel had curved and wandered and we could have easily swung through ninety degrees. In any case I didn't know the Ballarat streets well enough to be able to position the city above us.

We had broken in at two o'clock so it must now be around five or later. That could explain the cooler air, and it was getting colder. If it was getting colder we must be near some place where the cold air from outside could seep in. That would have to be an exit or a vertical air shaft.

"Look there!"

Suzie had spotted the change in the roofline first. In the distance the beam from the torch showed a break in the rock ceiling. There appeared to be a gap in the roof. As we came closer we could see a square cut hole in the ceiling. It must have been an air vent or an escape shaft for emergencies. But how to climb it and what would be at the top. I knew from my experience of mine sites these shafts were usually sealed off for safety reasons when the mine closed. Even if we could climb up, and I doubted my ability to do that, it would be shut off when we got to the top. Perhaps our phones would work and we could call for rescuers. I hoped they would come before the bad guys found us again.

When we shone a torch up the shaft it was better than I had hoped. The shaft was about three feet square and had been an emergency escape as well as an air vent. At the top there was a small dim patch of light. At least it was not completely sealed off. Stains on one side of the shaft showed where water had drained down the wall. Even better an old rusty ladder was fixed to one wall. If I could jump high enough I could grab it and pull myself up and then climb to the top. That would leave Suzie in the tunnel alone, and that would not be a good idea if our captors returned.

Better I lift Suzie until she could reach the ladder and let her lead, I could follow behind her. I only hoped the ladder was secure enough to take both our weights and hadn't rusted away near the top. I jumped and caught a rung, so far so good. It felt firm, so I climbed a few more rungs and swung on it. It still seemed secure. Dropping back onto the ground I explained my plan to Suzie.

Cupping my hands under her foot I heaved and felt her take her weight on the ladder. Suzie scrambled up higher and I jumped, grabbed a rung and we both started to climb. As we climbed higher in the dim light I could just see Suzie's feet above me. At last we reached the top. Our luck was in. Although the ladder was badly rusted and had a few weak treads, it was still strong and had been secure enough to support the weight of both of us. Suzie felt around the opening.

"There seems to be a heavy metal grate over the hole. I can't see or feel any catch."

As I expected the cover would be closed off from outside, probably from the time when the mine ceased working. These types of covers were made to stop people entering the shaft from the top, not exiting from below. Since I couldn't see past Suzie to check the grate I would have to climb up and around her, and she would need to come down a few rungs to give me space to try to work at finding some way of opening the cover or attracting attention. It would be a tight fit but we could manage. The closeness of our bodies as I climbed past brought back memories of our times together in London, and our more recent intimacies. Suddenly I found myself wondering what would happen if we were ever out of here.

Suzie's inspection was accurate. There was a heavy steel grate, however the spaces between the bars were too narrow to allow a hand to reach through. I could find no sign of any catch, either on the bottom, or, from what I could feel with my fingers through the bars, on the top. From experience a grate like this was probably welded or riveted in place to prevent anyone opening it. We were not to get out from this shaft.

Hopefully the phone might work now we were at the surface so I reached into my pocket for the phone. ooo answered. It must have seemed a strange call for the operator. Trapped in an old mining tunnel somewhere under Ballarat, someone was trying to kill us, come quickly. For operators plagued by hoax calls this must have seemed like a bad Saturday night.

"Where are you?'

I didn't really know myself, and I could expect little help from an operator in a call centre in Melbourne or some other distant place. I explained the tunnel from the basement of a building opposite the Grande Imperial hotel and linked under the road to the hotel. A side tunnel leading off that on the right or left depending on which direction you were coming from. The steel door on the side tunnel, but couldn't be sure it was the second or third door or if it would be open or shut. I explained the emergency shaft and told her we would wave a torch through the grate if we heard people above. I hoped that someone would come before daylight. As I looked down to tell Suzie what was happening I caught the flash of light on the tunnel wall below us.

"Quiet, I think someone is coming!"

Our only hope would be to stay as quiet as possible and hope that the shaft would be ignored. Trapped at the top of the shaft unable to escape we would be easy targets. If he had come back he would be sure to have another gun and maybe some help. He wouldn't know we had his gun but I was sure he would have looked for it when he entered the tunnel. When he couldn't find it he would suspect we had it. That thought should make him careful.

The flashes of light on the walls increased and moved past our escape shaft. He had either passed the shaft or must be very close to it. Then the light flashed up. He had seen the hole and ladder.

"Check up the shaft."

Unless he was giving orders to himself there must be at least one other person. The torchlight lit the shaft. We were in full view, like two trapped rats up a drain pipe.

"Come down or I will shoot you both!"

Our situation was not good. Any shot up the shaft would certainly hit either Suzie or me, possibly both of us, since we were locked so closely together. To go down would be to face death. Our only way was bluff. I waited until he started to call again and fired a shot. The noise filled the tunnel and rang in our ears. Four left, not good for a firefight but it might make him think about tackling us and bring us time. I hoped he wouldn't decide to hide out of our sight and just expose his hand when he fired a volley of bullets up the shaft. That surely would be the end of us. I had the feeling he was a bully, and like many bullies, lazy. He didn't want the effort of getting us down if our bodies remained hanging at the top of the shaft with an arm locked through a rung of the ladder. Much easier for him if we came down, walked to our grave and were shot. I was sure we were to be shot.

Our only option was bluff and there we had an advantage. My one shot had slowed him down. Now we had to convince him to leave.

"You're too late. The police are on their way." I hoped it was true. "It won't go well for you trying to explain our bodies because they know we are here."

"You're bluffing."

The answer was expected but it would have him thinking.

"The mobile works up here, we've spoken to the police. They will be coming into the tunnel from the basement. There are also teams looking for this shaft. They are looking for the light from the torch." Then I added the fact I hoped would have the greatest effect. "They know about the other bodies."

"Shit! What bodies? You didn't say anything about bodies." It was evidently the second man. He was finding the job more worrying than he had expected.

"There are two bodies in the side tunnel. The one with the rock wall. A man and a woman. Didn't your boss tell you about them? How will you explain that to the police?"

"Mate. Let's get out of here. I don't want no trouble with the cops."

"Shut up!"

"You had better listen to him. If the police find you in the tunnel you will be linked to those murders. Your only chance is to get out now. Any delay and the cops will have you."

I just hoped he wasn't a quick thinker and decide that he could empty the gun up the escape shaft and still have time to make his exit.

"Let's go mate. Let's go."

The fear in his companion's voice was insistent. The light at the end of the shaft disappeared. Had they left or not? We were too afraid to move.

We stayed huddled together clinging to the ladder and each other for what seemed like an hour. The closeness and warmth of Suzie reignited all the old memories from years ago. We didn't talk; fear still hung in the air.

The sun had come up before we heard voices above us. We shouted and shouted hoping that someone somewhere would hear our voices and find the shaft. The legs of a policewoman viewed through the bars of the grate was the best sight I had seen for a long time.

26 THE POLICE

Suzie

After all the stress and drama it was wonderful to have the company of another woman, even if she was on the far side of iron bars. I wondered how Peter would explain the situation to the police.

After warning about the two men with guns in the tunnel below, and giving directions to the entrance to the tunnels, emphasising the need for the police to cover both the derelict building and the hotel, he went quiet. I supposed it was the problem of the break-in that worried him. We were burglars. I decided it might be better if I explained the situation and avoided the details of what Peter and I had done. My story might distract the police from our break-in.

More police arrived after the radio call from our discoverers, but still we remained locked in the shaft. My arms were becoming sore from being hooked around the hard steel rungs of the ladder, yet we weren't confident to climb down in case the gunman and his mate were still there. The police effort to find someone who could remove the steel bars of the grate above our heads was not proving successful.

Finally we heard voices and noise from below. The rescue team had arrived.

We descended the ladder. Five men in bullet proof vests were waiting for us with guns at the ready. As we dropped to the ground we were grabbed and pushed against the wall. Somewhere in the communications the message had been confused. It probably didn't help that Peter still held a gun. After taking the gun from Peter they relaxed a little but still handcuffed each of us to a policeman. Our explanations had no effect. As we were going past where Merry and a man had been entombed I suggested they had better check the side chamber. When they saw the two bodies their confusion increased. Peter's message to 000 had certainly been poorly relayed. I was becoming concerned.

"Did you get the two men who were leaving the tunnel?"

"Yes, they said the alarm system had shown intruders in the old mine tunnels. They went to check but found nothing. They were in the first tunnel heading back to the hotel."

"Apart from shooting at us! I hope you still have them."

"They said they would wait until we returned. They should be in the hotel with some officers."

I thought to myself that it would be very unlikely that they would wait around to help the police!

When we got back to the hotel the officer-in-charge took us into the dining room which had now become a police command centre. At last I had a chance to explain what had happened. I could see Peter was worried about our breaking and entry so I skipped over those details just saying we had found an open window hoping the story of the murders would attract their attention. After that, minor trespass would not seem very important. I explained our suspicions about the gambling den and Merry's disappearance, the scuffle at the entrance to the side tunnel and how we had been locked in but found the gun the gunman had dropped on the floor. Then our search for a way out, finding the bracelet, and how our suspicions led us to pull down a wall across the side lead and find the bodies in the chamber.

It was an unlikely story and the policeman seemed unconvinced until one of our rescuers confirmed seeing the bodies. The officer-in-charge sent a man to fetch our two assailants. Unsurprisingly they could not be found. At least that added credence to my story.

Next we were taken to the police station. By now the media had heard of the situation and we were jostled as we left the police car. Shouted questions and cameras made those few yards from the car to the station mayhem. I wondered how politicians and celebrities coped with it every day.

The hours in the station passed slowly. Peter and I were separated and taken to different rooms to go over our stories and make written statements. I wondered how his entry to the tunnel would compare to mine. At least he could say it was an open window. No need to say he had broken it, and I wondered if the jemmy and screwdriver had been found and if they could be linked to us. I explained as best I could the disappearance of Merry and our suspicions. Hopefully finding two murdered people from forty-one years ago should be of more concern than possible squatters smashing a window and curious tourists interested in the interiors of old buildings.

At last Peter came back into the room. He looked tired

and I realised it had been a very long day and night. Now was midday. We hadn't been to bed for twenty-nine hours. We were alone again for once. I reached out to touch him and suddenly I wanted more. I wanted to feel him close, his arms around me.

As I moved in close and felt his arms around my back I felt pressure on my hip. The phone! I had the gunman's phone, the one he had used to make a call. It was obviously to his boss. The number would be in the history or call log. The police could track him down. The number could be tracked.

Peter was less certain. He doubted the number would be registered to the boss personally. He would just be a voice on the far end of a call. I took out the phone. It hadn't worked when we looked at it in the tunnel, but we had been preoccupied with the gunman's return so we hadn't wasted time on it. Besides, we had our own phones.

I looked at it and touched it. Nothing! Then I pressed the button to turn it on. It lit up. Was it locked? No! I touched the icons to try to find the history and finally there in front of me was the number. I was just prepared to call when Peter stopped me.

"Give me the number. I'll put it in my phone, that way the police won't link us to calling it when we give them the phone. They can do their own enquiries."

"Peter I want to talk to the man who killed my best friend. I want him to know we know."

"You will, but just wait until we are away from here."

Eventually the police took our story seriously and decided we were free to leave. They had confirmed my story of a young woman disappearing all those years ago. They had also decided we did not look the murderous type. Now they were looking for the manager of the hotel who had vanished, along with his mate. They even offered to drive us back to Melbourne. Then Peter remembered the borrowed car sitting in the street. It had been there overnight and all morning. It would have a parking ticket.

It did.

Standing next to the car we looked at each other. We couldn't face the drive back to Melbourne. Ballarat no longer held any pleasure for us; all we wanted was sleep. The first vacant motel we could find would do. We checked in. By now there was no question of how many rooms or how many beds. A bed to sleep in was all we wanted.

But first I had to make a phone call. I dialled the number.

"Yes."

"We have found her body!" I hung up.

27 THE DEATH OF BERNARD MAYNE

Peter

When we woke in the early evening Suzie turned on the television. The evening news was on. Television reporters were in a street in front of a high concrete fence with familiar wooden gates. Leading Australian businessman Bernard Mayne had been found shot dead in his Toorak mansion. He had been about to sign a major investment project with the State government to develop and build a huge new international hotel, apartment and office complex in the centre of Melbourne.

The TV showed the wooden gates closed off by police tape and the usual to-ing and fro-ing of police investigators and reporters. Police cars and vans and an ambulance were standing in the street, their lights flashing. Curious neighbours stood watching, puzzled by the unusual activity in the leafy green street where normally the only worry was the possibility of theft from very securely protected homes.

While police were saying they did not believe that there were any suspicious circumstances, the journalists were already reporting the death as suicide. There was no sign of a break-in at the house and it was rumoured in-house security cameras showed Mayne shooting himself.

His wife, speaking from their holiday house in France, told reporters that he had been anxious and unsettled in recent weeks.

The television report showed Mayne's son speaking of his father. Alexander Mayne was agitated and very angry as he delivered what could have been a eulogy to his father. He spoke of his father's rise to wealth and how he had contributed so much to the community in many different ways. He spoke of how great a loss the death would be to so many people and so many charities. His father had been troubled by a few people causing him great stress in recent weeks. Those evil people, who had caused his father's death, would surely get what they deserved.

His son's rant held some truth but ignored much that we had discovered about Mayne. I wondered how much his son knew. Did he really believe all he said about his father, or even know about the other side of Mayne's activities? In any case Mayne was dead. He would never face trial and what had happened to Merry would probably never come out.

Mayne, the poor boy from the bush, had died a wealthy man, but his past had caught up with him. His secret of the two disappearances, and the bodies at the Grande Imperial had been found out.

Our suspicion was that Billy had large debts from his gambling. Money he could never recover from the crooked tables at the Grande. The phone call he received was probably from Mayne demanding payment. His usual method, when necessary and if threats failed, was to arrange the kidnaping of wives or children of recalcitrant debtors.

They paid and the hostage was released. Normally nobody complained because it was all illegal and they did not want police attention. Merry had been kidnapped, and Billy got his phone call from Mayne. That was why he was travelling to Ballarat, not Melbourne. Anxious and driving too fast for the bad road conditions, he had lost control of his car and hit a tree on the way. When he spoke of a friend in trouble he must have been referring to his sister, and when he said he would sort it out, he must have been hoping to reach some agreement with Mayne—although how or what we would never know—then Merry would be released. With Billy dead Mayne couldn't let Merry go. She knew too much. That's when Mayne sent Slowgo to Sydney to be out of the way. Merry was killed, along with the Ox. Mayne must have realised that the Ox was unhappy over the treatment of Kempner and perhaps other jobs he was expected to do. His sister had told Suzie that her brother was planning to leave. The Ox knew too much and was a risk so he had to be removed forever. The bodies were hidden in the old mine tunnel between the Grande and the Gaming room and the entrance blocked off.

Probably Mayne had sold the hotel and office block to various companies he secretly controlled and then leased out the hotel to another publican. That would fit the nominee company holding we had found. Yet he always retained a controlling interest of the buildings. Perhaps it was like the way some people keep the first dollar they earned framed on a wall. Certainly it meant he could continue to hide his crime and control any attempt to demolish the buildings which might reveal his secret.

Finally, when he knew that the bodies were found, he must have realised that the government would never sign a deal with him. Probity issues could be managed over his sometimes dubious entrepreneurial activities, but once the bodies were found, and linked to him, his business dealings would be over. He had always been a gambler with high levels of debt. Everything he had was on the line. Everything he had built up would be lost, and once again he would be the poor boy back where he had started. He couldn't face that prospect and took the only way out he could see.

In a way he paid for his crime by losing everything he had accumulated, as well as his life. It was probably the sense of failure that must have been the greatest agony for him. Not the exposure of his activities, not even jail would be so painful. Now the knowledge of what happened would probably never become public, but at least the Oliver family and Dot would finally know what had happened to Merry and the Ox, even if it would hold little consolation for them.

The next story on the nightly news was about a house fire in Melbourne the previous night. Police were treating it as suspicious. The elderly occupants had still not been found. Then I saw Suzie start.

"It's my house!"

I looked again at the television. There in front of the house was the burnt wreck of what had once been a baby blue car. The front of the house was very badly burnt, and it was hard to see from the footage how much of the house remained. Certainly the house would need considerable work before it could ever be lived in again. Perhaps it would even need to be demolished completely. For the second time today I took hold of Suzie and hugged her. I felt her crying in my arms. At last she broke away.

"I must ring Max and Emma. They must be frantic with

worry not knowing where I am. And I don't like being called an elderly occupant!"

She made two long calls to her children. From the sounds of the conversation on the telephone I was sure that my situation was now even less favourable—especially with Emma.

28 DRIVING BACK

Peter

When Suzie tried to call her children she had found the battery of her phone was flat, so she used mine. After she had finished her phone calls we sat together on the bed and just looked at each other. Our afternoon sleep after leaving the police station hadn't really helped much and we both still felt exhausted. The dramas of the previous night and this morning, plus the news of Mayne's death and the house fire had left us drained: emotionally and physically.

Suzie told me of her children's worries. Max had seen the morning television coverage and realised the house fire was at his mother's house. He had rushed over only to find the fire extinguished and the house cordoned off with police tape. None of the neighbours were able to provide him with any news of what had happened, and the fire brigade had already left. He had contacted the police but again nobody was able to give him much information apart from the fact that there were no bodies found in the house. All he could discover was the fire was thought to be suspicious. There was no knowledge of his mother's whereabouts. He had tried phoning his mother but got no answer to his call. It appeared Suzie's phone must have been off all day due to its flat battery. Max had wanted to call me but didn't have my number. Then he had phoned his sister. Emma had not seen the television reports and was frantic with the news. She had also rushed to the burnt house and then joined Max at the local police station. This would have been about the same time we had first entered the Ballarat Police Station. A murder attempt and two bodies in Ballarat and a burning house in Melbourne were not linked together by the police in either Ballarat or Melbourne. Her children had tried calling Suzie all day, and phoned around her friends to see if anyone knew where she was. All without success.

The relief when Suzie had rung her son was immense. He was ready to drive up to Ballarat immediately and bring his mother back to Melbourne. She would have to stay with him and Amelia until something was done about the house. He was afraid it may have to be demolished. When Suzie told him of our experiences he was even more concerned. I think it only made him want to come even sooner and rescue his mother, but Suzie talked him out of it, promising to come to him first thing in the morning.

The call to Emma was different. She was exceedingly anxious about her mother. It was so unlike her mother to go missing, and to be in such a situation. I was obviously the cause. I felt my stocks decline even further. The more Suzie explained, the more I seemed to be at fault in Emma's view. It was unlikely I would ever get Emma's approval! She would be waiting at Max's house when we arrived back in Melbourne. I did not expect a friendly welcome from her.

When I went to make two cups of motel coffee we realised that apart from a coffee at the police station earlier in the morning we hadn't eaten for twenty-four hours. We decided to find a fast food takeaway. Any sort would do. We were in no mood to dine out. Just grab something and come back to our room and sleep. We found a fried chicken shop just before it closed. At least that filled a need. Then we fell into bed together. All we wanted was sleep.

I had a restless night. I kept thinking of what could have happened. Every time I woke I could sense Suzie was still awake beside me. As soon as we could we paid our account at the motel and started our drive back to Melbourne.

Within a minute Suzie decided on a change of plan.

"I want to go to Creswick. I must see Dot O'Hartigan and tell her we found her brother."

Suzie

Dot O'Hartigan was sitting in the same chair in the same sunny corner of the nursing home lounge. When she saw me she smiled in recognition. I thought her smile will soon fade when I tell her our news, but I was wrong.

"I knew he must be dead. All these years. He would have come back and seen Mum and me. Frank wouldn't have stayed away, but thank you for coming. At least I know for sure."

Merry's death was premeditated. Mayne had to kill her because he knew she would go to the police if he released her. The Ox was different. I couldn't see someone dragging his body along the tunnels to his final resting place. Perhaps he had gone with Mayne and then realised what was to happen to Merry and tried to prevent it. Dot believed her brother was a good man. I wanted to think that at the end

Merry would have died with someone trying to protect her, even at the cost of his own life. Mayne was dead. We would never know.

Peter was very quiet as we drove back to Melbourne. Neither of us spoke much. My thoughts were on Merry. What were her final moments? I knew that was her who lay thrown roughly into that small lead tunnel like some bag of rubbish. I was alternatively sickened and angry. Such a waste. Someone so full of spirit and life. Someone who only saw the good in people. Someone who was such a good friend.

I had made another phone call before we had fallen into bed the previous night. It was to Meredith Oliver. I told her of our discovery and promised to come down as soon as I could. I wanted to warn her of what we had found before it became public knowledge. At last she would have closure.

Then there was Peter. My thoughts turned to those years long ago in London. I had been attracted to him then. So much so that I had run away. While it had been fun to be with him, I had thought life with him would lack excitement. Maybe it would have, but from the way he spoke he had had an interesting life with a wife who had supported him, and lived with him in the remote mining camps. Would I have made such a good partner? I don't know that I could have adjusted to such a way of life. Claire had, and he still spoke very fondly of her, and their son was obviously close to his father.

Unlike my life. My kids were close, Max and Amelia and little Charles, and my daughter Emma, but my marriage hadn't survived for long although we had gone through the motions for years. I had dreamt of an exciting life and exotic places. London in the seventies and Tony had offered that, until his womanising had caused the marriage to deteriorate. My attempts to restore the initial emotion and romance were ignored by his need for variety.

Once Max and Emma had finished university they ventured out on their own, and eventually both moved to Melbourne where my parents lived. At least they had the opportunity to spend a few years knowing my father before he had died. My mother had loved the company of her only grandchildren, and they made my parents' house their base until they moved to their own apartments. With both of them living in Australia, England seemed empty, and I had soon followed them. Back home in Melbourne I had picked up with old friends and met new friends and remade my life. Now I was a grandmother. I wondered if I would ever be a great-grandmother. My mother had been one for three weeks before her death.

Again I thought of Peter. I had thought life with him would be uneventful and dull. What would it be like to be his wife? For someone I thought would lead a dull life the last few weeks had far more excitement than I wanted. Car crashes, threats, breaking into buildings, house burnings, being shot at. That was not me. I decided to turn the car radio on to try to change my thoughts.

A song I vaguely remembered was being played.

"That seems very appropriate for us."

I looked at Peter.

"It's 'Riders on the Storm'. The Doors. It seems appropriate the way our last few weeks have been. It was a big hit when we were in London."

The next track the station played I knew. Roberta Flack. The words had frightened me back in London. I recalled the first time I ever saw Peter. It was part of the reason I had fled. I was afraid that the words would prove too meaningful. Even today the words still troubled me. I felt the same way. Would I flee again or would I accept what I felt? I didn't know.

"You're very quiet."

His voice and his face made me realise I wanted to be with this man. All those years ago in London it was more than friendship. It was love. That was what had frightened me then, and even now, in the short time we had been together, I still longed for the feel of him, his closeness and warmth. We hadn't been exactly chaste after our first few nights sharing a room, but it was what I wanted. He had always been the gentleman and I had provided the encouragement.

Where did we go from here? Would he go back to Sydney and out of my life? Would he come to Melbourne and move in with me? He could hardly move into my house considering the fire. Perhaps we could rent until it was repaired. What did he feel? I knew he found me attractive, certainly in a physical sense, and we did enjoy one another's company. How could I ask him what he would do? Me, who was usually so organised and forthright. I didn't know what to say. I wasn't even sure what I wanted. Did I want to go with him to Sydney? That would mean leaving my children and grandson. I would miss the most important people in my life, but I would miss Peter if he left. I had never had the feeling for someone as I had for him, not even for my ex-husband in the early days.

As we approached the outskirts of Melbourne I made two

decisions. First, I must go down to Oakleigh tomorrow. I had to tell the Olivers what we had found before the details made the newspapers and television. Peter agreed to come with me. There was a second thing I wanted to do. Roley was back in town. He had left an open invitation to phone him for lunch or dinner. I would take it up. It would be a dinner he would never forget! I knew I was avoiding another decision—Peter.

Peter

Suzie was very quiet on our drive back to Melbourne. I guessed it was more than just the relief of our escape and knowing what had happened to her friend. We had become very close in the few weeks since our meeting at the National Gallery. Perhaps it was just the events that engulfed us but I suspected it was more. Once we had been lovers with a special bond, and that old feeling had re-emerged, at least it had for me. I thought Suzie also felt it, but could I ask her to leave her family and move to Sydney with me? I knew how much they meant to her. If she stayed in Melbourne we could visit each other, commuting between cities and homes. The cost would not really be a problem but it was not the sort of relationship I wanted. Perhaps I should move to Melbourne. I loved my home that I had built with Claire. But was that really important? If she moved to Sydney it would solve the immediate problem of the fire damaged house in Melbourne. Then there was Matthew. I was sure my son would not object to me starting a new relationship. Perhaps I should fly over to Western Australia and see him. It was a year since we had last had the opportunity to spend time together, and it was coming up the anniversary of his mother's death. I hoped he would approve of Suzie when he met her. What did Suzie want? We hadn't discussed it. Perhaps it would be best to let things settle and see what happens. For both of us. I would miss her company. I decided I would book my flight home for when we returned from Oakleigh and the Olivers.

Suzie

When we arrived at Max's all my family were waiting. Max and Emma jostled to hug me. Amelia, with Charlie on her hip, waited back a little, the small boy looking puzzled by the unusual behaviour of the adults. We sat in the lounge room and I told the full story of our adventures, or misadventures. Max was relieved to know that it was all over. Emma still held Peter fully responsible. I could see that would be an ongoing problem if I decided to live with Peter.

Almost at once the decision was made that I would move in with Max and Amelia. Their house was only small but it did have a tiny third bedroom that they used as a store room. If they tidied it I could use it as my room until something was resolved about my house and the fire. The tiny room and the single bed cut short any question of Peter staying with us. That seemed to please Emma. Peter, with his usual tact, offered to book into a nearby motel. That way he would be close for our trip to the Western District the next day.

Peter

Our immediate problem was clothes. In our haste to get away we had left for Ballarat and our planned break-in with only the clothes we were wearing. After our drama in the tunnel they were no longer clean and we had been living in them for what seemed like days. Suzie's clothes and all her memories and personal treasures had been burnt in the fire. All she had were the clothes she was wearing and a spare toothbrush which she kept at Max's house. At least I had not lost everything in the fire. I had only brought a few clothes with me on my return from Sydney and they could be easily replaced. All I needed now were some new underclothes, two shirts and a pair of pants. I decided a heavy jacket might be useful with the cold weather forecast for the next few days. My greatest concern was the loss of my laptop computer. I hoped my back-ups were up-to-date, but I dreaded the thought of re-installing all the programs and reloading my files. A new computer would have a new operating system, and I would have to learn the new system. The process could take days. It would be an experience I was not looking forward to.

My problems were small compared to Suzie's. She wanted to see her house and asked Max to drive us there before we went to the shopping centre. As we stood looking at the remains of her home I was expecting her to cry at the sight of the burnt wreck of her home but she had no tears left. I was confident the house would be covered by insurance, 'Little Miss Organised' would have made sure of that. At least she would have some financial support to rebuild her life, but still there would be the emotional loss and all the decisions that would have to be made. By the time we arrived at the shopping centre neither of us was in the mood for buying clothes but we had no choice. Practicality would have to override pleasure. We made our selections and left as quickly as possible.

When we returned to Max's I decided it would be best if I gave the family time together. I still had to return the borrowed car to my friend. It would take some time to explain all that had happen while we were using the car, and to sort out the parking ticket. I wondered if Rob may have already seen us on the nightly news.

Suzie asked if I would return.

I answered, "Tomorrow."

29 RETURN TO OAKLEIGH

Suzie

The drive to Oakleigh was a sombre affair.

I knew I had to visit the Olivers and tell them what we had learnt. It was a task I was not looking forward to, but I felt I owed it to the family of my first best friend.

Even the dark grey car Peter had hired seemed to fit my sombre mood. My lovely yellow convertible was still in the repair shop. The parts that were coming from overseas were still 'coming from overseas' and the car was still not ready. I had also had an interesting time explaining to the car hire company that 'Baby Blue' was fire damaged and could only be returned on a trailer. We would have to discuss that problem when I returned to Melbourne.

Peter was driving. Usually he was always interested in the scenery or what was happening outside the car, but today he drove, saying nothing, lost in his thoughts. I turned on the radio but soon turned it off. I looked for a CD but we hadn't brought any with us. We drove on in silence.

Our news would bring closure for the Olivers. Although I

knew that many years ago, even before Merry's father had died, her parents had accepted that she must be dead. I had spent many happy holidays with them and seen the love in the family. Merry would never have run off and left her parents with such uncertainty.

Now Billy's anxious and withdrawn moods on his return from weekends away fell into place, as did Merry's concern about his behaviour. They had been close as brother and sister, and while she may not have been aware of his gambling, or his losses, she knew something was wrong. Jane Oliver's remark about the family's concern over Billy's spending and his constant demands for more money now made sense. Even their confusion over a missing cash payment for the sale of some wool just before Billy died could be explained.

As soon as Bernard Mayne's suicide became public knowledge stories of his activities and financial interests, past and present, spread rapidly. It became the subject of the day at many business lunches and private meal tables. People who would never before discuss him, either for fear of his business influence or their physical wellbeing, spoke openly. More information about his businesses dealings emerged, including some which were highly questionable. Tentacles of his empire reached out far wider than previously known, often hidden behind nominee companies or through financial arrangements giving him ultimate control without public knowledge. Even his current dealings were not always legal or ethical. It was rumoured that the whole business empire might collapse.

Stories also emerged of his early days in Ballarat and the illegal gambling room. Stories that told of visits from unpleasant men and threats of violence. Violence that eventuated if the gambling debts were not paid. If threats or bashings did not produce the money then kidnapping followed. Merry had not been the only abduction but she was the only one not to be returned. Whether she was grabbed from the street after leaving her office or talked into visiting Ballarat under the pretence of helping her brother we would never know. Billy's car crash was a complication. Mayne would not have wanted him dead, he wanted the money, but now Mayne had a problem. He could not release Merry and be confident of her silence. The only way he could be sure of her silence was to kill her, and he knew of plenty of old mineshafts for the body. That still left the abductors. Slowgo had been lucky to be sent away and never return. The Ox was not so lucky. With all the witnesses gone Mayne was free to continue, but police enquiries about gambling made the risk too great so he had shut the casino and moved to Melbourne. The timing was fortuitous. Australia was growing rapidly and he grew with it, but no matter how much success he had, there was always the secret buried in Ballarat.

I had arranged to arrive at Oakleigh early in the afternoon so we could start our drive back to Melbourne later in the day. Peter had booked his flight to Sydney for two days' time. We would only have two days and nights. One night would be back in Melbourne and I would be in the single bed at Max and Amelia's, Peter at the motel. Peter had suggested we stop off on the way back to Melbourne and promised me dinner. I had agreed depending on when we left Oakleigh.

Once again we sat in the familiar drawing room, the wood

fire burning in the open fireplace. Sitting on the chintz-covered lounge I had first seen on my school holidays so many years ago, surrounded by many of the same paintings and ornaments from those days, the violence and unpleasantness of the past weeks seemed like an unreal nightmare.

Customary country hospitality dictated cups of tea even given the sadness and significance of our news. Meredith and Jane served tea and scones as I told our story. As I expected we were invited to stay the night, but once I had answered all of Meredith's questions I wanted to make our farewells and start the drive back to Melbourne. I had finished the story and we were reliving old times when my mobile phone rang. I excused myself and went into the hall to answer it.

It was Max. He was anxious. Amelia and Charles were missing. They had gone for a walk in the park and had disappeared. He had gone to the park looking for them but they were not there. When he returned to the house there was a message on the door. 'You interfered. Now you will feel the loss.' He had already contacted the police who were on the way to see him. I went back to the drawing room and explained the call. Peter took my hand and we left.

As we drove away I wondered if I would ever return to Oakleigh. I wasn't sure that I could again face the sadness in the eyes of that gracious aged mother who had lost two of her children. At least now she knew what had happened. I wondered how I would cope in such circumstances. It was something I hoped I would never need to discover. With Max's news I had a horrible feeling I was going to find out.

The drive back to Melbourne was an even more sombre affair. I was worried by Amelia and Charlies' disappearance, and I could see Peter shared my concern. This time it was not the sunny scenic Great Ocean Road of just a few weeks ago, but the main highway with its traffic and trucks. All we wanted to do was get back to Melbourne as quickly as possible.

Suddenly I started to shake. Peter looked at me.

"What's the matter?"

"That smell! It's the smell I smelt when the truck tried to kill me."

I looked in the mirrors but there was no white truck.

"It's pigs. The semitrailer up front has a load of pigs. That's what the smell is. Haven't you smelt pigs before?"

Pigs. Of course. It's years since I have had anything to do with them and that was only my father's porker for the Christmas ham. Like many on the land in those days he kept a piglet to feed on surplus milk from the house cow and to eat the kitchen scraps. It was a big day when the pig was killed and the hams and bacon pickled or cured.

Coming closer to the semitrailer the smell became more intense. What I had smelt when the white truck had stopped to check the accident was the same smell but not as intense.

"Why would the truck that tried to run me into a tree have smelt of pigs? It was a tip truck."

Another part of the puzzle fell into place. When we had first gone up to Ballarat in the train we had seen a white tip truck unloading topsoil or mulch at the new housing estate.

The estate developer was Grande Developments, Bernard Mayne. He also owned a landscaping supply company. Landscapers used pig manure as fertilisers in their blends. It all tied together.

30 INVESTIGATIONS

Peter

It was dark by the time Suzie and I arrived at Max's house. We were met by a police woman. Max and Emma were waiting for us inside.

We heard the story from Max. Amelia had taken Charlie for a walk and a play in the nearby park. When they hadn't returned by midday Max had phoned Amelia on her mobile but there was no reply. Then he had gone looking for them. They weren't to be seen but he had found the stroller abandoned in the street. Puzzled, he returned to the house with the stroller and had phoned some of Amelia's friends thinking she may have met up with one of them and gone off for a coffee. Nobody had heard from her. He phoned Amelia's parents. They had not heard from her either so he decided to walk to the local shops to see if she had gone to the supermarket, and on the way he had another look around the park. When he returned to the house Amelia and Charles were still not there but there was a message pinned to the door. He phoned the police and then his mother.

When the police arrived they had questioned Max and

searched the park. The park was only small and the search had not taken much time. The police had questioned a number of walkers and joggers in the area but none had seen either the missing pair or Max. One woman recognised a photo of Amelia having seen her in the park on other occasions, but had not seen her that day. It was hardly surprising. Amelia, Charlie and Max would have been in the park much earlier in the day.

The police had taken possession of the message Max had found and carried out a search of the house. It had been written on a sheet of A4 paper. The standard type used in most offices and home printers. The writing was a scrawl in black texta, again something found in most homes. Max had noticed the police take a sheet of paper from his printer and place it in a plastic bag. They had also searched through his desk.

I remembered once reading an article on murders. Apparently you were more likely to be murdered by someone you knew, often someone close to you, than by a complete stranger. I suspected the police were working on the same theory. Max seemed to be the main suspect. I hadn't known Max for very long but I just could not see him as a murderer. From the little I had seen of the family they were a loving couple and devoted to their child.

The second theory of missing wives was that they had run away from unhappy marriages, perhaps with a new lover. Again I didn't see that as likely. The police search of Max's house had not found any indication to support the theory. Amelia's and Charlie's toothbrushes were in the holder in the bathroom. None of Charlie's favourite toys appeared to be missing and nor was any of Amelia's clothing missing. Neither Max's phone call to Amelia's parents, or a follow up visit by the police to her parents had given any indication of dissatisfaction with the marriage or plans for leaving home.

As darkness closed in the police had called off their park search and decided to put out a missing persons alert on the evening television news. We had not seen it driving back from Oakleigh.

Next morning the police were back in the park. This time they were questioning people who were more likely to be in the park around the same time as Amelia and Charlie had disappeared. Again they had had no success until a woman walking a little Sydney silky terrier mentioned seeing a woman and child getting into a white van. She thought the men were helping them. It had seemed strange because they drove off and left the stroller behind. At least that confirmed Max's story. The woman had been on the opposite side of the park and had not had a good view of the people. Another police search of the area where she had seen the van found a tiny blue train lying in the gutter. Suzie said Charlie loved his blue engine.

The white van triggered a thought. The house must have been watched. Someone must have seen Max go to the park and pinned the sheet of paper to the door while he was away. It would be unlikely to be someone from the white van with two abducted people held in it. I wondered if there had been a black ute in the neighbourhood. Or a green car. Why would it be the same white van? Mayne was dead. There are lots of white vans. At least I did have a photograph of the white van parked outside Suzie's house on my phone. Maybe the police could get a number plate from the photo. It was worth a try.

The television announcement had not brought any assistance from the public but the number plate of the white van had been more helpful. Police had traced the owner, a Sam Michaels, to an apartment in Brunswick but he was not at home. Further enquiries had discovered that he worked in the building industry, although neighbours had said his work hours were very irregular and they were never sure what exactly it was that he did. Police had put an alert out for the van and the driver.

Yesterday the police had either Max as the chief suspect for doing away with his wife and child, or else Amelia had run off with a man. Today's theory was drug debts. Did anyone owe any money? Did we use drugs? Again it seemed an unlikely cause. Max and Amelia didn't seem to be into drugs. I certainly wasn't. Even at university I had stayed well away from any sort of drug, apart from alcohol. I had never seen any indication that Suzie was a user, but then I didn't know what may have happened after I left England. She certainly didn't give any indication of drug use in the time I had spent with her lately. It seemed another pointless line of enquiry.

In managing men on mine sites I had often considered what I would do if I were in their situation. Putting yourself in another person's shoes gives you a different view of life. Why would I want to abduct a woman and a child? How would I do it? The how was obvious. Wait till they were alone, preferably in a quiet place where nobody would notice. Pull up alongside them when they were walking in a quiet street and ask for help. An accomplice could open a van door to ask where they were on a map. Then the driver and accomplice could bundle the woman and child into the van, close the door and drive off. Watch them, and pick the time and place and it would be easy. But why? That was harder.

There had been no ransom demand. That would be an obvious reason, but neither Max nor Suzie really looked like ready money. Comfortable, yes, but not the sort of people who would have bags of cash under the bed. Perhaps it was a mistake. They picked up the wrong people. That thought was frightening. The knowledge of what had happened to Merry was still fresh in my mind.

The other reason could be hate, or revenge. They were much the same. Who would hate Max? He seemed a likable fellow. I couldn't see him with enemies. Perhaps it was Suzie? Mayne had certainly been behind an attempt on her life but he was dead. He could hardly organise a kidnapping from the grave. Then I remember his son. He had an angry, almost psychotic manner when we had seen him on the television. In that interview he had threatened the evil people who had caused his father's death. Perhaps he wanted revenge. He certainly appeared to have a personality problem. We needed to find out more about Alexander Mayne.

Suzie suggested a dinner with Roley. She had already planned to tell him very forcefully that she was not impressed with his connection with Mayne and the trouble he had caused her. He had known Mayne for many years so he would probably know his son. Suzie didn't really think Roley was a bad person, he just conveniently overlooked the bad in others. Instead of her taking issue with him for the trouble he had caused, perhaps he could be of help. It was unlikely that he would approve of kidnapping children. Suzy decided to call him and arrange dinner.

While I struggled on the computer to cancel my flight back to Sydney, Suzie phoned Roley. From the snatches of conversation I overheard, Roley had suggested a quiet restaurant two nights hence. Somehow that had been changed to a dinner tonight, at a very expensive restaurant favoured by the local establishment. Not only that, he would send a limousine to pick up Suzie at six forty-five and to return her after the dinner. She was sure he would sort out any problems organising a car and getting a reservation— even if the restaurant was fully booked. When she put down the phone Suzie looked at me and smiled. She had certainly worked Roley over. It was a side of her I had never seen or even suspected. 'Miss Organised' certainly had management skills. I almost felt sorry for what was going to happen to Roley tonight.

31 THE FUNERAL

Peter

The newspapers had been full of stories about Bernard Mayne. Representatives of various groups had called for a state funeral for the man who had been a benefactor to so many organisations and causes. Politicians, arts administrators and sportsmen were vocal in their support for such an honour. Yet for some reason the government had remained silent. Still a big service was planned at the Cathedral, with the Archbishop leading the Mass and dignitaries and businessmen from across the country expected to attend.

On the day of the service all the television channels showed coverage of the Mass in their news segments. A long line of black cars waited behind the hearse at the main door of the dark grey gothic revival cathedral. The Cathedral itself was filled with an assortment of people. Bankers and business leaders rubbed shoulders with building workers. Footballers stood next to artists and performers. While many politicians and senior bureaucrats joined the throng somehow the top political leaders of all parties were away in other states, 'their absence due to important commitments which they had been unable to reschedule—junior members of Parliament would represent them'.

In the television coverage little attention was given to the eulogy by Mayne's son. Alexander Mayne had given a long, strange and rambling speech on the company and the great deeds his father had done for the people of Australia. While the television reports showed a few seconds of his speech the cameras mostly concentrated on the rich and famous attending the service. Discussions held in bars and offices around the city by those who had attended the service were much more frank. Opinions ranged from 'weird' to 'what planet is he on.' After eulogising his father's deeds the son had then described his father as becoming weak and out of touch. It was he, Alexander Mayne, who knew how the business should be run and he had continued by listing the changes he would make, the people who would be replaced.

The financiers who had been in the church were unimpressed, the art organisations saw their income vanishing and the building workers were bemused and puzzled. However all got the message. It would be advisable not to interfere in the new Mayne operation.

The following day newspaper articles began to hint that some politicians were starting to distance themselves from any Mayne connection. Rumours had begun spreading, suggesting that bribes had been involved in some of Mayne's dealings. Messages were also circulating that some very embarrassing stories about Mayne were soon to emerge. Bankers were thought to be discussing the future of several projects and new equity may be needed to replace debt. It would probably require new partners to be brought into the ventures. The newspapers that had yesterday published glowing tributes about Bernard Mayne today published large sections of Alexander Mayne's speech, although even these were highly edited and it was only in a few commentaries that Alexander Mayne's more curious statements were reported—including the threat that those who had caused his father's death would suffer.

32 DINNER WITH ROLEY

Suzie

I had chosen the restaurant because I was sure there would be diners there who knew Roley. My belief was correct. He was waiting for me, whisky in hand, talking with a couple he obviously knew, when I stepped out of the restaurant lift. He introduced me to his friends and we chatted together admiring the lights of the city stretching out far below us before parting to our separate tables. As the maître'd ushered us to a table I felt Roley's hand on my back, just a little firmer than was needed. When the wine waiter came to take our order I chose a very old, very expensive, French vintage champagne. I thought I saw a small look of concern when Roley realised the price. Tonight was going to cost him much more than a night out with his usual lady friends. Normally I prefer French sparklings from other regions of France, or from the smaller producers around Epernay than the wine from the big Champagne houses. They also suited my purse much better, but tonight I would go for the best, or most expensive. I smiled and told Roley tonight was a night for celebration. I would let him into the reason later.

Over the entrees we made small talk. Roley told me of his

latest visit to Hong Kong and the changes to his house in Thailand. I let him talk, asking questions so I didn't need to tell of my doings. Like most people a few questions at the right time and he was happy to talk. As the waiter cleared away the plates I mentioned my recent visit to the Western District to see the Olivers. That gave me the chance to bring up the subject of Merry and Billy. Roley again had recollections of Billy and a vague memory of the disappearance of a young woman from the streets of Melbourne but had never put the two events together.

When the main courses arrived I told him of my latest experience. He already knew of my previous visits to Ballarat from our earlier lunch, and my phone call, but I updated him on my arranged road accident and the firebombing of my house. I told him of my last visit to Ballarat and our finding of bodies in the tunnel. I told him of the attempt on my life by the gunman. I must admit I did downplay Peter in these matters. Then the definite link to Mayne and his subsequent suicide. I also told him I knew he had been the one to tip off Mayne. I could see Roley was shocked. While he knew Mayne was not always squeaky clean, and occasionally used force, he had never thought that it would go as far as murder. His attitude to the legality of some of his clients actions had always been relaxed, but murder was one step too far. I continued to chronicle Mayne's bad deeds and how he, Roley, would be implicated in them. He protested that it had nothing to do with him but I pointed out how his connection with Mayne's businesses through Hong Kong would look in the newspapers. The link was there in the financial reports should a journalist wish to investigate.

Over the Wagyu beef infused with the flavour of saltbush and a beautiful old red wine from the Coonawarra, I brought up the main reason for the dinner. Alexander Mayne. Roley would know him from his father. What was he like? Roley's description confirmed the comments I had heard earlier in the day when I had phoned friends I thought may be able to advise me. Mayne's son was the spoilt brat of a wealthy man. He was not thought of as very smart but traded on his father's reputation. An arrogant man with a bad temper, he was used to the good life with little consideration for anyone else, including his current wife who tolerated his behaviour and girlfriends for the lifestyle benefits she enjoyed. I did feel a twinge of guilt at that thought. He was also considered to be a bully and there was a suspicion that he enjoyed hurting people. I suspected he might be the young man who had visited Kempner and Belmond.

Mayne junior had a taste for toys: fast cars, motor bikes, a speed boat and jet-skis at the holiday house. I decided we would go ahead with the plan Peter and I had worked out earlier in the afternoon. I was sure Alexander Mayne was behind the kidnapping. We would reverse the situation.

I offered Roley a chance to redeem himself. He was to go to Mayne and tell him about a friend from Hong Kong who had a car in storage in Melbourne. It was an old Ferrari GTO 250. Did he want to have a look at it? Roley's friend had sent it to Australia when he planned to move here but circumstances had changed, it was rumoured his business was going bad. Now he had to stay in Hong Kong and was going to return the car back to there. He might even have to sell it. Roley was to say his friend was possibly desperate for some quick cash. It was to be all very vague. Anyway it would be a good chance to see one of these cars—they were a rarity. I hoped the bait of the iconic car would interest a boy who liked expensive rare toys. The thought he might be able to buy it cheap from someone desperate for cash was an added attraction.

Roley agreed to make the phone call. I think he was genuinely troubled by the news of the two bodies in the old mine shaft. He might be a sleaze and prepared to overlook bad behaviour but deep down he was a decent person. I even gave him a kiss on the cheek as I entered the limousine and was driven away. By the time I arrived at Max's house our plan for Alexander Mayne was underway.

33 ALEXANDER MAYNE

Suzie

The more time that Amelia and Charlie were missing the greater their danger and our fear. Unfortunately we could do nothing until nightfall arrived. We would just have to wait, and hope all would be resolved without any harm coming to them. For Max and Emma and me the day seemed endless.

When I had returned from England I had bought a warehouse unit in Tullamarine. I thought the location close to the airport and a freeway would make the warehouse a safe investment and provide me with a regular income. The income had been reliable and sound until my last tenant. The real estate agent who handled the lease had described the tenant as a young go-ahead businessman involved in imports from China. All had gone well until one day the rent wasn't paid and we discovered the lessee had disappeared. When I visited the unit with the real estate agent another story emerged. Apparently our clean-cut young man had lots of friends with motorbikes and tattoos. The police were also interested in my unit and there was a strong suspicion that not all the imports were legal.

After we had finally cut our way into the unit with an angle grinder we found it had been substantially modified behind the façade. It was fitted out with security cameras monitoring the exterior and interior, the doors were now operated remotely and had been strengthened. The place had become a fortress—or a prison.

As arranged, Roley had phoned Alexander Mayne who fell for the bait. It may have been the day after his father's funeral but the son wasn't so grief-stricken that he couldn't look at a possible new toy. Roley agreed to accompany him to the unit to view the car. Then at the last moment he had rung to say he was delayed but gave Mayne the address and said he would meet him there as soon as he was able to get away from his meeting.

It was nine o'clock at night when Mayne arrived at the warehouse in his red Ferrari. It fitted what I had heard about his character: that he liked to show off with his expensive cars, and prove he was part of a rich boy's club. I had hoped he would come alone, but as Peter had expected he was accompanied by a man who had spent a lot of time in a gym developing his muscles. When Mayne pressed the button on the intercom to announce his arrival a voice answered. We doubted he would recognise Peter's voice over the intercom.

"Yes?"

"I've come to see a car."

"Who are you?"

Peter and I were watching a screen in an office inside the building. Mayne was used to giving orders, not to being questioned.

"I'm Alexander Mayne. Roley Donaldson arranged for us to have a look at a car. He is coming later."

"Oh yes, alright, come in. Perhaps you had better get your man to put your car in the loading dock. We have had trouble lately with graffiti artists tagging cars parked around here at night."

The large roller door started to rise, a light came on over the steps leading up to the offices and a door opened. The voice on the intercom told Mayne to come up the steps.

Mayne spoke to his companion and 'Muscles' went to fetch the car. We were confident Mayne would not want teenagers doing a paint job on his showy red car. As he walked up the stairs a door shut behind him and the light went out momentarily. The big roller door on the loading bay closed. When the light came back on Alexander Mayne was trapped and his car had disappeared off the street.

Mayne tried the next door. It was locked. Becoming concerned he rushed back to the first door calling for his bodyguard. He found this door was also locked. No amount of force by either Mayne or his man would open that door. The bikies had done a good job with their security and the remote controlled locking.

"I'll call the police." He pulled out his mobile phone.

"You do that. They are already looking for you. They will be very interested in finding you. You and your friends in the van."

"Van? What about the white van?"

The way he asked about the van confirmed our suspicions—he already knew about it. It wasn't really a question about the vehicle but more about how much we knew about it.

"POQ 362."

"I don't know anything about it." The answer came too quickly to be convincing.

"Try Sam Michaels. Does that help?" The police had told us they were searching for him as the owner of the van.

"I have a friend coming here. He will be looking for me."

Peter lied. "He has had a change of plans. He is flying out of the country right now. He didn't want to be around to answer any questions the police may have." It all sounded very convincing.

"What do you want?"

At last we were getting somewhere. Up to now I had been terrified that Mayne may have been innocent. How then would we explain our actions? If he wanted a deal he must have been involved in the kidnapping, although I didn't see him as doing it himself. He would use some of his father's connections. I only hoped we would not be too late. The people I had spoken to in the morning had been adamant that Mayne was a bully who liked to humiliate and hurt people. I was sure he would want to enjoy the pain he was inflicting on us and not rush to kill Amelia and Charlie even if he wanted their deaths as revenge for his father's. He would want to savour the anxiety he had created and keep them locked away until he had decided our family had suffered enough. Then I was sure they would be killed. Just like Merry.

"We will do a swap. You for them."

"What do you mean?" It seemed he had decided to play innocent again.

"You will never leave here alive unless the woman and child are returned to their home. You have one phone call, don't be smart. It is your life or theirs."

I thought Peter should have had a career in the movies. He was playing the heavy so well.

"Phone your mate in the white van. Tell him to return the woman and child to the house where the note was left. Tell him to do it immediately. When we get a call to say they are safe you will be released. Any funny business and you and your mate are finished!"

"He may not answer."

"You had better hope he does!"

Mayne took out his phone and called a number. I was terrified that he might say or do something that would harm Amelia and Charlie. Would our bluff really work? At last he spoke and issued an order. Now we only had to wait and hope it would all work.

"Can I go now?"

It was a cheeky request that was certainly not going to get a positive reply.

"No, you wait. Place your phone in the top drawer of the cabinet now and move to the far door."

Mayne complied. The bikies had conveniently built a double sided drawer in the cabinet. Probably to facilitate the transfer of cash and drugs. It was useful to remove any temptation that Mayne may have to make another phone call.

Now we had to wait. The minutes seemed endless, the hours an eternity. Without any furniture in the room Mayne had taken to sitting on the floor. His arrogance had disappeared as he sat hunched in a corner. The cool night air in the bare, unfurnished room made the wait even more unpleasant.

Having agreed to the swap he eventually became more communicative. Probably it was the boredom of the wait, and the fact that he had admitted to organising the kidnapping. Peter softened his tone and began asking questions. Mayne replied, almost with a tone of bluster. He wanted to show how clever he had been, and how capable he was. His father ran the business but he, Alexander, took care of the inconveniences. He was almost boastful about it. I could see he would enjoy his work, it was a game for him and he took pleasure in hurting those who crossed him. I was sure he was involved with the bashing of Kempner and Belmond.

As he talked I recorded the answers on my phone. I didn't know if it would be admissible as evidence in a criminal case but it would give police something to work with. I hoped they would overlook our restraint of Mayne. After all he had entered voluntarily. I was sure a smart lawyer would find a loophole but I would have my family back together. That was all that was important to me.

As he talked he admitted to arranging the white truck that ran me off the road. It had been a man who worked for the landscaping company. He had also arranged the house fire after one of his men had found the note. His father was getting old. He lacked the drive to run the business anymore. Now things will be different. Our suspicion about Roley was correct. He had passed a message on to Mayne senior who had become concerned that his old crime might become public. Mayne still controlled the Grande Imperial in Ballarat through the nominee company. The publican had orders to make sure nobody ever looked in the tunnels. Mayne junior had paid off the gunman and his mate from the hotel. They were safely in Bali, out of the way, but they were useless, he would never use them again.

I wondered about Alexander Mayne. In some ways he seemed to live in another world. All his confessions were unimportant to him. He just didn't realise, or perhaps care, what they could do to him. Other people meant nothing to him. Perhaps he trusted us as fellow criminals who felt the same way and would just forget all that had happened. Possibly he believed that with his money and access to expensive lawyers he was untouchable.

At last my mobile rang. It was Max. Amelia and Charlie were home.

I phoned the police.

31 DECISIONS

Suzie

Peter was concerned about how the police would respond. He thought they would take a very dim view of our actions, after all we had basically kidnapped Mayne. We had also recovered Amelia and Charlie while they were still searching for them. That wouldn't please them either.

While I was on my phone calling the police, Peter was phoning the television news rooms. He hoped they would arrive before the police.

We still had a problem with Mayne. He was securely locked in the entry room of the warehouse, but that was between the room we were in and the personnel entry door to the unit. Police would meet him before they reached our little office deeper into the unit. That would not be to our advantage. We decided to let him move back to the loading bay, his car and his minder. They would still be safely imprisoned but we would have access to the front door for the police. Flicking a switch Peter unlocked the door to the loading bay. Mayne heard the click but was unsure what it meant. Peter spoke into the intercom.

"You might be more comfortable waiting in the car with your friend. You can go through the door."

Mayne moved very cautiously. He was unsure what his extra freedom might mean. Once he had gone through the door it swung shut and the lock clicked into place again. It reminded me of working in the sheep-yards with my father when I was a child.

Watching the monitor in the office we saw Mayne and his man try the main roller door. They would have little joy with that. Only an angle grinder or an oxy torch would give them freedom. On the other monitor we saw the police and the first TV crew arrive at the same time. The police did not look pleased with their company. We unlocked the front door and over the intercom invited the police into the unit. The TV cameras tried to follow but were held back. Once the officers were inside we moved to meet them. Our story was met with incredulity. They were a patrol sent to respond to the call and had only a general idea of the situation. They radioed for advice. We were to remain where we were and not talk to the media. Then they went to Mayne.

Once he saw the police Mayne's whole manner changed. His bluster returned and he demanded we be charged with kidnapping. He demanded his lawyer be called. The poor police officers became even more confused. He was also told to wait until the detectives arrived. That made Mayne even more irate. Fortunately the officers had the sense to keep us apart. Meanwhile more media crews arrived and could be seen on the monitors, their vans filling the carpark.

At least the detectives had knowledge of the abduction and phoned Max to confirm the safety of Amelia and Charlie. They were not happy with the media scrum outside but there was nothing they could do about it. They were furious with Peter and me and were going to arrest us, but Peter pointed out how bad that would look in the media. Did they want vision of a grandmother in handcuffs when the story emerged that she had rescued her daughter-in-law and grandchild when police had not succeeded? How would the police look with news headlines, 'Grandmother rescues stolen grandchild while police dilly dally'? I handed over my phone with Mayne's confession. After they had listened to the recording, Peter offered them a solution. First we wanted to see my family, then we would report to whichever police station they required later in the day and make a full statement. When we left we would make a brief statement to the media expressing relief the pair had been recovered and thanking the police for their assistance. We hoped that by the afternoon their bruised egos would have recovered. That still left the problem of Mayne and the lawyers he would no doubt have on the case. His confession on my phone had registered with the detectives. I doubted even with his money he could escape from what he had said.

It was around two o'clock in the morning when we arrived at Max's house. The lights were still on, and when we entered my whole family was there, only Charlie was in bed asleep. The others had not been able to settle down and were sitting drinking coffee waiting for our return. Emma and Max hugged me and Max took Peter's hand. Amelia, who was still looking drawn, came and hugged both of us. Then she burst into tears. Finally she found release from the drama and fear of the last two days.

Until that moment she had remained strong for her little boy.

They had been grabbed from the park as we already knew, then taken to a building somewhere in the suburbs. She had no idea where. She had been blindfolded. She thought the van had parked in some sort of industrial unit and they had been locked in a room. The building may have been a panel beating or spray painting workshop. There had been a strong smell of paint and solvents. They hadn't been treated roughly, and were given food and drink. The coffee was terrible and Charlie had been given fizzy drinks. There was a mattress on the floor and they had some blankets. She had no idea what was happening and what it was all about, but she knew she had to be brave for her baby.

Once we were settled Peter went to leave. I walked to the car with him, and when we reached it I put my arms around him and kissed him. I had so much to thank him for.

"When will I see you again?"

"Later. Don't forget we have a date at the police station."

I watched him drive off wanting to be with him, but my family were waiting inside.

The statements to the police were straight forward. We told the whole story, starting with the gambling, Billy's car crash and Merry's death. Our enquiries, and the attempt on my life. The arson attack on my house that should have left us dead. Mayne's involvement and death, and the revenge abduction. For once all the pieces came together. The sense of relief as we left the police station was immense. At last it was over. On the way back to Max's house Peter told me of his plans to return to Sydney. Would I come with him?

In the past few days I had realised how much my family

meant to me. The thought of not being with them was too much. I couldn't leave them. I wanted to be with them and watch Charlie grow up.

Peter came to say goodbye next morning. We parted when the taxi arrived to take him to the airport. A gentleman to the end Peter gave me a hug and a kiss on the cheek and got into the taxi. As he was driven away I felt a loss. I had enjoyed his company and having him close by. I had enjoyed the intimate times we had spent together, and as the taxi disappeared around the corner I knew I would miss him.

I had my life, my family and my friends. "Get on with it," I said to myself.

The phone rang. It was Peter just letting me know that he had arrived home safely. Neither of us said much. I busied myself around the house with Amelia. Nothing had been done for days because of the kidnapping and a fine layer of dust had settled over everything. Out with the vacuum cleaner and dusters. A friend who lived in the bush where there was a lot of dust once made a sign to hang in her house which said 'This house is protected by a layer of dust'. We lived in a city with sealed roads and paths and we didn't have the excuse of dusty roads and stockyards. At least the cleaning gave me something to do to take my mind off Peter.

Next morning I woke, still thinking of him. It was the weekend. Max and Amelia, Charlie and I went for a walk in the park, but now there was a feeling of unease. The park would never be the same again. Charlie was having fun playing on the slide, untroubled by his experience, but we adults were edgy and unsettled. Doing some shopping with Amelia I realised why we have our babies young. As beautiful as our little dark-haired boy was, I was exhausted and so pleased to hand him back to his mother when we stopped for a coffee break. Emma phoned to check on me and we all ended up having dinner at Max's. Around the table I could sense that they were anxious about me. Although they had met him they were puzzled by Peter and our relationship. I decided that I owed it to them to explain our history.

I had sometimes wondered how my kids would take a new man in my life. I knew they had very mixed feelings about their father. Since moving to Australia they had had much less to do with him. Max was certainly more like me but I could see something of my ex-husband in Emma. Perhaps that explained why she had never settled into a long term relationship. I was never sure if it was because she was too like her father, or if she was avoiding the mistakes she had seen me make. Both of them had made it clear they did not approve of Tony's string of girlfriends.

I returned to look at my home. I loved my house with its little garden. The neat entrance with its winding path of bluestone pavers. Perhaps not ideal for high heels, but since I wore them only rarely these days that wasn't important. I had loved the gabled roofline with its warm red tiles, and the large windows which let in the winter sunlight. Now it was a burnt shell and unliveable. I would have to find an architect and builder to see what could be saved and repaired, or perhaps even demolish it all and start again. I sat amidst the ash and rubble in the little side courtyard with its Japanese maple and prunus, both still alive but leaf-less and scarred from the fire. It was my favourite place in the afternoon with a coffee or glass of wine and a book. The backyard had space for Charlie to run around in when I baby-sat him. The elm tree would be ideal for climbing when he was bigger.

My mobile rang. I answered, but it was not Peter. It was Elizabeth Holmes, my old friend from schooldays. It was her husband, Ian, who had put me in contact with Roley. She had heard the news about Ballarat and wanted to hear of Merry. Apparently Emma had phoned her that morning and suggested she have a coffee with me. We arranged to meet for lunch at the Botanic Gardens. The Royal Botanic Gardens is one of my favourite places in the city. Elizabeth and I had often met there and strolled the gardens in the different seasons before having coffee in The Terrace. It was just across the road from The National Gallery where I had met Peter over a cup of coffee before our adventures had started.

We met, as arranged, at the gate near The Shrine of Remembrance. Our wandering took us around the edge of the Oak Lawn. The leaves of the oaks were just commencing to turn but it was still too early for the full effect of their magnificent colours. Our path led us on through the Fern Gully and past the viburnums. At last we came to the Ornamental Lake with its waterbirds and the restaurant. We found a table outside in the sunshine. Nearby on the lake the seagulls and water hens scrambled and scrabbled while two black swans sailed elegantly between the varied ducks. Beyond the water the lawns and gardens were a multitude of shapes and textures in so many shades of green.

"What's this about your man?"

As usual Elizabeth was direct and to the point. Emma must have told her of my adventures, or misadventures, with

Peter. I hadn't mentioned him when we had spoken in the morning.

I corrected her. He was not 'my man'. He was an old friend I knew when I first went to London.

"Does he live in Australia?"

I explained that he was Australian and lived in Sydney. His marriage, his work, and his wife who had died.

"Emma said you were very unsettled. She thinks he has got through to you. She has checked him out."

I thought how times change. Once upon a time I would screen Emma's boyfriends to see if they were suitable. Not that it made any difference. She did what she wanted. Now she wanted to screen my friends. Not that Peter was a friend. He had left and I had my life, my family, my friends and my house. So why was I unhappy?

Elizabeth chatted on about mutual friends, parties that were coming up and the usual girl talk.

"Do you think Jane is losing weight?"

"What?"

"Is Jane losing weight? I don't think she is eating well. She is talking about some new diet."

I realised I had not listened to any of the conversation. My mind was in Sydney thinking about Peter. What was his house like? Even after our time together I really still knew so little about him, and yet ever since he had left he had been on my mind. The cleaning, the garden, the kids, even today with Elizabeth I was really trying to prove that he didn't mean anything to me. But he did.

Elizabeth saw my distraction. "Emma thinks he must be special to you. Is he?"

"She doesn't seem to like him."

"That's not what she told me. Apparently he fails her social sensitivity test but she thinks he is a good man and he would make you a great partner. She is a smart girl, she knows you. What are you doing about it?"

"Nothing."

Again I went over the past few weeks and explained we had separated, if you could ever say we were really together. How Peter had returned to his life in Sydney and I to mine in Melbourne.

"Suzie, I have known you since schooldays. I've seen your boyfriends, I went to your wedding. I would even have warned you that it was not a good idea to marry Tony but I knew you would not have listened to me. I have a good feeling about this one. Don't lose it."

That night at Max's, lying in the single bed I thought about Elizabeth's advice. In the morning I phoned Emma. We met at her apartment. It was a long talk. A mother/daughter talk, and a talk of two grown women and their lives and loves. We talked of fears, and we talked of issues we had only ever partly resolved. It was a long day and an emotional day for both of us, but by evening I had made my decision.

I phoned Peter's home number.

"I'm not available at present, please leave your name and number and I will call you back."

I tried his mobile.

"The number you have called is not available. Please try again later."

I called the home number again.

"Peter, this is Suzie. Please call me."

I waited two days but no answer came. I tried his email. The message was sent and did not bounce back. A week later still no call. I phoned again, again the message. I became more concerned. I was sure he would have replied—regardless of his feelings.

It was as if he had disappeared.

I booked my flight to Sydney.

I had to find him.

Links:

Some of the locations mentioned in the story exist in reality and are open to the public. They are well worth a visit.

Readers seeking more information may wish to view the following websites.

National Gallery of Victoria	www.ngv.vic.gov.au
Kimberley Art	www.kimberleyfoundation.org.au
The Great Ocean Road Drive	www.visitgreatoceanroad.org.au
Ballarat Tourism	www.visitballarat.com.au
Sovereign Hill	www.sovereignhill.com.au
Craig's Royal Hotel	www.craigsroyal.com.au
Ballarat Begonia Festival	www.ballaratbegoniafestival.com
The Whitsunday's	www.tourismwhitsundays.com.au
Cloudehill Gardens	www.cloudehill.com.au
Puffing Billy Steam Railway	www.puffingbilly.com.au
State Library of Victoria	www.slv.vic.gov.au
Royal Botanic Garden—Melbourne	www.rbg.vic.gov.au

About the author   www.valverdemaclean.com

For readers interested in the songs played on the radio a quick search of YouTube will find:

"Maggie May" by Rod Stewart

"Chirpy, Chirpy, Cheep, Cheep" by Middle of the Road

"Riders on the Storm" by The Doors

"The First Time Ever I saw your Face" by Roberta Flack

This page intentionally left blank.

ABOUT THE AUTHOR

Valverde Maclean has a passion for Australia.

He has travelled widely throughout the country and has lived and worked in both the southern and northern regions of Australia.

His interest in the Australian history, particularly the development of the inland, and the ramifications for the economic life of the nation are a background to his stories.

He is also very interested in the present day changes and challenges to Australian culture.

He presently lives in Queensland, Australia, near a small village, in the beautiful Sunshine Coast Hinterland.